GOD SENDS
SUNDAY

GOD SENDS SUNDAY

A NOVEL

ARNA BONTEMPS

WASHINGTON SQUARE PRESS

NEW YORK LONDON TORONTO SYDNEY

WASHINGTON SQUARE PRESS
1230 Avenue of the Americas
New York, NY 10020

ISBN: 0-7432-6891-1

First Washington Square Press trade paperback edition February 2005

1 3 5 7 9 10 8 6 4 2

WASHINGTON SQUARE PRESS and colophon are registered trademarks of Simon & Schuster, Inc.

Manufactured in the United States of America

For information regarding special discounts for bulk purchases, please contact Simon & Schuster Special Sales at 1-800-456-6798 or business@simonandschuster.com

To P. B. Bontemps

— PART ONE —

I

AS A CHILD, ON THE RED RIVER PLANTA-
tion where he was born, Little Augie was not
required to chop cotton or work in the rice
swamp like the other boys of his age. He was considered too frail for hard labor. Instead it became
his duty to mind the cows when they grazed in
the clover fields and to lead the horses to the
watering-place.

Augie lived with his grown sister, Leah, in the
same quarters in which he had been born shortly
after the 'Mancipation and in which his old dead
mammy had been a slave. He was a thin, under-
sized boy, smaller for his years than any other
child on the place, and he had round pop-eyes.
But he enjoyed a certain prestige among the
black youngsters, and older folks as well, because
of the legend that he was lucky, a legend that

had attended him since birth, due to a mysterious veil with which he had entered the world.

Set apart from his mates by these circumstances, Little Augie soon grew to be miserable. In his heart he felt inferior to the strong, healthy children who worked alongside the grown-ups in the fields. He became timid in the presence of unfamiliar people and fell into the habit of stuttering when he tried to talk.

Sometimes, to amuse himself, Augie would follow the men out to plow the fields and then ride the horses home for them in the evening. It pleased him to sit on the back of the old lead mare and watch the other animals string along behind. It made him feel good to be directing the procession, shouting at the tired critters and giving the orders to start and stop. So, as he grew older, Augie spent more and more time with the animals. He became a competent rider. Curiously, he did not feel timid when he was riding or managing a fine horse; he felt big. And he loved horses for that reason.

Augie had also one other diversion. He liked to watch the river boats that came puffing around the bend and past the plantation now and again. Especially was he fascinated by the *P. T. Blain* that came on alternate Wednesdays, because it was the one that stopped at the tiny wooden landing in sight of the quarters. Augie had never been on hand to see it dock, but he had often watched it from the big barn gate where, sitting on the top-piece, he could see everything plainly—the rousters loading and unloading barrels, the old white captain with the mutton-chop whiskers, and the black loafers standing along the plank in the sunshine.

One spring morning, however, his chance came. A young heifer that Augie was about to stake in the clover field suddenly kicked up her heels and started down toward the river, the chain and stake dangling behind. Augie had to follow her till she became tired of running before he could get his hands on the chain, and when he did he realized that he was a long way from home. Returning, he saw a crowd of folks at the landing, and his heart leapt. It had not occurred to him that the day was the second Wednesday, but there was the *P. T. Blain* splashing and booming against the piles.

Augie climbed a stack of boxes and sat with

the heifer's chain across his arm. He was speech-less with pleasure. Wouldn't he like to ride in a boat like that! Folks said it went to New Orleans, but that was not important. He could not imag-ine such a boat going anywhere that was not infi-nitely desirable.

The rousters worked rapidly. A loud-mouthed crew, they drew the attention of several oily-faced young women who stood by, giggling. It was a sight to watch those half-clothed men at their work; ascending and descending the plank, their movements suggested cats. The fine elastic muscles slipped loosely under their skin and their moist bronze shoulders glowed like metal. When they were finished they promptly went aboard and withdrew the plank.

The captain looked down at Augie and the heifer from the little upper deck. The *P. T. Blain* was about to push off. Augie called to him:

"High there, Mistah Steamboat Man!"

"He-o, bubba," the captain said pleasantly.

Augie felt all the loafers on the landing look-ing up and taking notice when the captain spoke. The steamboat man had high-balled Little Augie! From that day his destiny was determined.

All through the lazy summer months that followed, Augie had visions of sailing away on the river boat, going some place down the line, maybe to New Orleans. He was convinced that he could never be a rouster, so that was not in his mind. He only wanted to travel. But the chances were slim and the urge wore off as the hot weather passed.

The next spring, however, it returned stronger than ever. Warm days came early. The road became dry and dusty, and the dust powdered the young blossoming trees. Augie watched for the regular coming and going of the freshly painted *P. T. Blain.* Each time he heard its whistle he would climb the gate and talk to himself till it pulled away.

"O Mistah Steamboat Man! Take me 'way from heah. I got de itchin' feet. Take me 'way away."

A small red rooster, a pet of the quarters, sat beside him on the cross-piece. Of the two sitting there, one seemed about as discontented as the other, but only Augie complained—even to himself.

"Gonna leave you heah one o' dese days, Red

Man," Augie said to his companion. "Gonna leave you heah, an' it might be soon."

That spring the mornings were diamond-bright. The fields, rippling and undulating with daisies, seemed to flow down to the river. In the cool dewy grass a glossy crooked-horned cow stood knee deep, tethered to a stake. A short distance away a young star-faced mare grazed with her dappled colt. Black men, naked to the waist, could be seen working small skiffs along the farther edge of the water.

One morning when he had finished his chores, Augie was lying in the deep wet grass, watching a host of blackbirds in a flowering plum tree, when suddenly a familiar sound, like the lowing of a gigantic steer in the swamp, rose near the horizon. The colt, amazed and trembling, whimpered and drew nearer its mother.

"Well, dog ma cats!" Augie exclaimed. He had lost the days again, and the *P. T. Blain* had slipped up on him. He jumped to his feet, forgetting the animals he was minding, and ran down the grassy slope. Climbing a rail fence, he got on the road and hurried along, his bare feet kicking up a white cloud of dust.

A score of idle niggers were on the landing when Augie got there. But they were not too soon; presently the clean white boat rounded the bend and came into full view, its enormous side-wheel splashing handsomely. A few minutes later it banged against the creaking piles of the landing and the rousters dropped the plank.

Augie stood apart in his miserable rags while the crew did its work. The captain, coming to the deck, noticed him.

"He-o, bubba," he called in his amused voice.

"Howdy, Mistah Steamboat Man," Augie answered.

Nobody paid any more attention to Augie. But, miraculously, when the *P. T. Blain* pulled off, the youngster was aboard. He was down in the hold, sitting on a pile of wood, his eyes round with fear and happiness. An echo of his own words, his own wish, kept going through his mind:

"Take me 'way from heah, Mistah Steamboat Man. Take me 'way away."

II

LITTLE AUGIE BELIEVED IN CONJURE AND
"signs." Having been born with a caul over his
face, he was endowed (he believed) with clairvoy-
ant powers. For example, he was able to see spirits, he could put curses on people and he could
remove them, and, above all, he was lucky—
unfailingly lucky.

Moreover, as a youngster, he had seen a "jack-
ma-lantern" in the swampy woods, and that had
also helped fix the course of his life. Augie
believed that he was bound to wander all his
natural days, that there would be no rest for him
any place until he had exhausted his luck and
met the final disaster that awaited him. For a
jack-ma-lantern was an unreal light, a brightness
that appeared in the dark thickets and swamp-
lands, that seduced its victims by leading them

on and on to destruction. The usual victims were men caught after dark in the woods, and the end was generally direct and speedy, but in Augie's case it had not been the same. The jack-ma-lantern that he saw came out of the pine woods after nightfall, hovered along the fence near the quarters, then traveled off toward the swamp. Augie had been playing alone under the clothes-lines in the back yard of Leah's cabin. A few pieces of washing were still up—outing flannel nightgowns, woolen shirts, and stove-pipe draw-ers, things that had failed to dry in a single day. At length, resting on the cabin steps and study-ing, it occurred to Augie that these clothes, swollen by the wind, looked like hideous old people. Maybe, he thought, hants had jumped into Leah's long drawers and filled them out like that. Maybe that was a witch in her nightdress. Then sure enough, he saw that it was so. He saw the long bony feet of the spirits, their hollow faces hanging over the lines, and their terrible hair blowing. He knew that it was because of the caul that he could see these things, but when the jack-ma-lantern suddenly appeared, he took that for a "sign."

Arna Bontemps

When Augie had been in New Orleans three or four days, he remembered these sights. He had fallen into a group of other young black wastrels and tramps and had spent the time loafing on the water front. He had picked up a plenty to eat, but he soon missed the comforts of Leah's cabin. So one morning he decided to venture away from the levee. At a pier where a tropical fruit boat was being unloaded, he begged some bananas; filling his belly with a few of these and his pockets with the rest, he set out on an adventure across the town.

Augie wandered all morning, and in the afternoon he found himself at the old Fair Grounds. He had finished his bananas, and he was hungry again. There were very few people in sight. Augie sat under a tree to rest.

"I feels ma luck comin' down," he told himself. "I's hongry, got holes in both ma pockets an' nowhere to go. But I sho is lucky. I was borned lucky; any nigger whut picks up wid me gonna be glad he done it."

A little later he drifted over to the stables where racing horses were kept. Augie timidly inched his way to a door and looked in. An old bald-headed Negro with a clubbed foot was standing in the stall nearest the door, vigorously rubbing a beautiful steaming animal that had just been exercised. The lean, proud horse kept his head raised triumphantly while the stableman worked on him; his tail twitched nervously. Augie was thrilled. He had never seen such a beautiful creature. He could feel his good luck coming down.

"Is dat yo' hoss, Mistah Bad-foot Man?" he asked suddenly.

Seeing Augie for the first time, the old Negro grinned, his curled lips disclosing a line of soiled teeth, most of which were gold. Augie confronted him in the sunlit frame of the doorway. . . . A tiny black youngster in a pair of ragged blue overalls and a red jacket. His hat was only the crown of an old felt hat (into it diamonds had been cut to keep his head cool), and his little gingerbread face and round eyes were alert and appealing.

"Nah, bubba, he ain't zactly mine. But I's got chawge o' him."

"He is one mo' beauty, I mind you," Augie said.

"Hm. You lak him?" The bad-foot man paused

to wipe the perspiration from his own brow. "Whose boy is you?"

"I b'longs to ma grown sista, Leah," Augie said. "But I done run off and lef' her up de line."

"Is you fixin' to go back?"

"No, suh, not presently."

"How come dat?"

"I gotta keep movin'. I wants to see de country."

"Oh."

"Could you, please, suh, let me ride dat putty hoss a lil piece, Mistah Bad-foot?"

"You is too lil to ride a sassy hoss lak dis, son. Dis is a race hoss."

"Oh!" Augie whispered. *A race horse!* "Yet an' still I b'lieve I could mind him, was you pleased to gimme a ride."

The bad-foot man laughed with admiration. "Come on in heah wid me, son. You is a mannish lil nigger. When de head man come back I'll see can I get him to let you have a shawt ride on one o' de hosses."

Augie and Bad-foot Dixon went down the stable together. They passed through an aisle of horses' tails and hind legs. The odor of the clean animals appealed to Augie. He had loved the old critters and mules up on the plantation—he worshiped these perfect creatures. He knew in his mind that this was the place for him.

"I done come home," he said to himself. "I'm gonna stay heah wid Bad-foot an' be a race-hoss man."

All that afternoon he wandered through the vast, well-kept stables in a dream. And in the evening Bad-foot carried him away and gave him a home. Augie promptly became a favorite of the men who were regularly in and out of the stables—the Negro jockeys, the trainers, the rubbers like Bad-foot, the exercise boys, and even the wealthy white sportsmen who owned the horses.

He grew to manhood among them, first as a sort of mascot and later as a stableboy. He followed the retinue to San Antonio and to Louisville and Mobile as the racing seasons shifted, and learned to amuse himself like the other Negro hands, drinking whiskey, gambling with dice, and clog-dancing. Augie could sing too, and in his spare time around the stable he learned to play an old accordion that he found there.

Arna Bontemps

The horses to which Augie and Bad-foot were assigned belonged to Horace Church-Woodbine, an irresponsible banjo player, the scion of a wealthy family of horse-fanciers. Augie became young Woodbine's special pet, and whenever the latter came to the stables he gave the boy a half dollar and ordered him to dance, young Woodbine picking the chords and calling the breaks. The young white man was loud-mouthed, slightly alcoholic, and good to his niggers. And Augie knew precisely how to put on a show to please him.

"Where's ma black boy?" he would boom, coming into the stable. Augie's small head would emerge from one of the stalls.

"Heah me, Mistah Woody."

Then as Horace Church-Woodbine strummed, patting his feet on the board floor, the boy would perform. Often, too, he sang.

> Oh, de jack won't drink muddy water
> An' he won't back off.

Augle's singing voice continued to run into the falsetto register—though in reality he was

nearly full grown—thus accentuating the child-
ishness that always characterized him. He looked
tired, despondent, and helpless when he sang.

> *Oh, de boat's gone up de river*
> *An' de tide's gone down.*

One spring in the early nineties, the fancy
Woodbine stable was hard pressed for jockeys,
and Augie was put into the saddle to fill the
need. Augie had looked forward to just such a
day since the afternoon, then years past, when
he had first wandered across the city to the Fair
Grounds. He had come a long way to those dim
sheds, and it had taken many years to achieve his
dream after arriving. Now, he thought, jack-ma-
lantern or no jack-ma-lantern, there would be
nothing further to attract him, no further interest
to draw him away.

On the board that afternoon there was the following item: "Number 7, Jennie Rose, filly, 2
years, Church-Woodbine owners, Little Augie
up." A dozen beautiful horses filed to the barrier—glossy black fillies, roan and dun stallions,
with little ink-spot jockeys, their knees buckled

high in their tiny saddles, in the monkey-on-a-stick fashion, resplendent in bright shirts and shining boots. Augie had drawn the outside position. He wore the broad red and white stripes of the Woodbine house proudly, but he seemed nervous as he waited, as was also his young brown mount.

There was a hushed pause, then the signal. The finely trained animals broke sharply. Augie's eyes were two large white lights in his tiny black face. A shudder of delight passed over his body. Suddenly something cut him across the face, and in the same instant he became aware of several horses pulling ahead of him. This brought him out of his trance. He thought of his own whip and the responsibility of winning the race if possible. This was more than a joy ride. And he realized, from the lash he had received, that there was a grimmer angle to the business, an angle that he had failed to consider. He put the whip on Jennie Rose. She strained her ears forward. Then, one by one, she broke the hearts of her rivals, running past them with a burst of speed that thrilled Little Augie like a vision of heaven.

Glancing back, he saw the crestfallen pack bat-
tling for the second and third positions. He
stroked his young filly tenderly and flashed into
the stretch.

III

BECOMING A JOCKEY WAS SIGNIFICANT to Augie's life primarily because of the curious transformation it promptly wrought in his character. With horses he gained a power and authority which, due to his inferior size and strength, he had never experienced with people. From the time of his birth, Augie had never been a participant in the life around him; he was the perfect mascot. As he grew older and became more keenly aware of his position among his fellows, his timidity had increased. But after he became a full-fledged jockey he was a new person. He began immediately to walk with a superior air and to carry his hands insolently in his hip pockets instead of at his sides. Plug tobacco no longer satisfied his taste; he started smoking cigars. And he set his mind on the women folks.

One afternoon, before the boys in the stable had become accustomed to the transformed Augie, he suddenly burst upon one of their crap games in a vacant stall and asked to join. Badfoot was in the circle, kneeling childishly, his slick head glistening with jewels of perspiration. At first he was too absorbed to notice Augie; another of the stableboys, however, waved the youngster away.

"Nah, son," he said, "dis ain't no penny-pitchin' game. There's sho nuff money in dis pot."

Augie ignored him. "Whut's de point?" he asked.

"Run long, small change, us ain't yo' size."

Augie snatched a half-dozen greenbacks from his pocket. "I'm in," he announced. "An' if dis heah buzzard says I ain't, I'll give him fo' bits to put me out."

There was no more back talk; Augie stayed in. Attended by his customary luck, he finished with a hog's share of the money. That was the beginning of his gambling. Forever afterward, Augie was conceded to be a great one with the bones. It was the second way he found to make himself feel like a big man.

Shortly afterward, Augie went with the Woodbine stable to San Antonio for a turf season there. It was the first trip he had made as a regular jockey. There were to be five weeks of racing, and Augie was to ride for a percentage of the purses he won in addition to his salary.

The races proved to be nothing above the ordinary, but to Augie the season seemed fabulous. He had never dreamed of so much money. He counted his earnings by the hatful. He carried money in his shoes, in the crown of his hat, in the lining of his coat, and in rolls suspended from his neck, under his shirt.

"I'm jes' dirty wid money," he told Bad-foot. "I got greenbacks on me worser 'n a dog got fleas."

"Whut you gonna do wid it all?" his old friend asked.

"Gonna take it home an' give it to de women folks," Augie told him.

"They is plenty womens in dis man's town too."

"Where they live at?"

"Down yonder by de I. & G. roundhouse."

"Sho nuff? Is there any spare parts?"

"Yea, Jesus! There is mo' fas' womens down yonder den ole Pharaoh had in de land of Egypt."

The Negroes of San Antonio called that neighborhood—which was the old red-light section—the "I and gin." In the heart of the district there were two blocks of odd shanties, all joined by a continuous porch, a single platform extending the entire length of their fronts. It was to one of these that Augie and Bad-foot came.

Augie was impressed by a big yellow woman named Parthenia. He sat with her in a small room that reeked of musk and cheap perfume and tried to give a big impression of himself. He had to keep fighting off the fear that she would laugh at him, that she would think him childish; for he was no more than half her size. He paid for a bottle of whiskey and then threw his change into the waste basket. He burned a bill over the kerosene lamp, lighting a cigar.

"You is a putty lil papa," Parthenia told him.

"Wha, wha! Well, I's jes' as bad as I is putty," he said. "Po' me anuther drink."

Before leaving her, Augie got thoroughly drunk, provoked a quarrel, and blacked both her eyes. She did not fight back. He had been generous enough to forestall that. Instead she pretended to admire him for his brutality. Augie left her, feeling like a giant. He stumbled out of the place and off the porch and wavered proudly down the sagging street. Bad-foot met him a few doors away and took him in charge.

Parthenia did not leave a very fine memory in Augie's mind, and he oddly imagined that all the "I and gin" women were like her. So he did not return to her shack that season. Instead he saved his money, as he told Bad-foot, to blow in New Orleans when they returned.

Another circumstance, too, restrained him for the time being. He had noticed that he was plainly dressed for one of his profession. Compared with the macks and sports he met, Augie was nothing to blind the eyes. Yes, he would wait, he repeated to himself, till he reached New Orleans again, and then he would spruce up.

"I's gonna git me a two-gallon high-roller hat dat won't do," he mused. "Gonna git a box-back coat an' a milk-white ves' wid red roses painted on it."

And true to his word, when he got home to New Orleans, Augie set about immediately to adorn himself for big killings among the women folks along the line. And since he had a taste for the gaudy exaggerated finery of sports from the honky-tonks and bordellos, he soon became a treat to casual eyes. His high-roller had tiny naked women worked in eyelets in the crown. His shirts had two-inch candy-stripes of purple, pink, green, or orange, and the sleeves hung so low they covered his knuckles. The cuffs were fastened with links made of gold money, and just below them on Augie's third finger a rich diamond flashed opulently. His watch charm was a twenty-dollar gold piece, and his shoes had mirrors in the toes and dove-colored uppers with large pearl buttons.

As a final touch, Augie had his eyeteeth drawn and gold ones put in their places. The operation was extremely painful, as every one knew; so if there had been any lingering questions about Little Augie's real manhood, this probably dispelled them. People, with the exception of Bad-foot, began to find it harder and harder to get along with him. He was a lucky little nigger, they said, and his luck had run to his head; he was getting biggity.

Augie quit passing time with the ordinary poor-mouthed blacks; he decided to identify himself exclusively with a fancier crowd—macks, pimps, gamblers, prize-fighters, and other jockeys like himself. He declared, furthermore, that no black women were for him.

"Black womens is onlucky," he told Bad-foot. "They is evil too, lak black cats. I wouldn't spit on one was she on fire."

In New Orleans, this time, Augie got his first taste of adulation, the first young fruits of fame. Strangers pointed him out on the street corners and in the bars. Young bucks enjoyed being seen in his company. In the barber shop where he and Bad-foot spent much of their time, he was the center of attention.

Among the social functions to which he was invited was a nineteenth-of-June picnic given by a group of church folks. For some reason Augie went. The picnic was to be held in a wood a number of miles from town, wagons and carriages being provided for the noisy crowd. Curiously, the sinners, guests of the outing, seemed to be in authority. Somebody crashed an empty flask on a wagon wheel before the procession started, and later other flasks were broken and the young people became gayer and noisier.

At first the church girls, in their gaudy summer dresses, overawed Augie. He had never been inside a church and he did not know how to behave in the presence of girls who had religion. He rode between two of them on the way out, a long cigar in his mouth, but saying little. His eye was really fixed on a tall yellow one riding alone in the back seat of another carriage. She wore a hat that suggested a summer parasol, and under it Augie could see that her mouth was painted. Her clothes were of a quality unlike that worn by the other young women. She stood out like a sunflower among daisies.

The boys of the crowd were mostly rounders and sports, invited from the streets. And being self-respecting bucks of this stamp, they carried their fighting-tools—knives, brass knuckles, razors, and, in some cases, pistols. The fellows who carried firearms were spotted early. They were the ones it wouldn't do to fool with.

As the carriages jogged along, Augie leaned

back and studied the group. Two notoriously dangerous boys were making passes at the fine yellow girl; one was Joe Baily and the other Tom Wright. Joe Baily, Augie knew, was the worst boy in his family, a family of twenty children, half a dozen of whom had been killed, and as many more were serving time. There was no doubt that Joe Baily was a bad nigger. Tom Wright, a more subdued fellow, was equally dangerous. He had a thin handsome face and a sunken chest; folks said he was "in decline." And the proof that he was bad was that he had already killed a man. Augie had a speaking acquaintance with each of these boys, and he respected them enough to suppress his own interest in the yellow girl for whom they were contending.

Later in the afternoon, when the time to begin the return drive to the city was nearing, a small group of the young people wandered surreptitiously into the woods in pairs. They climbed a small rise, went over a broken fence, and came down a slope, laughing and shouting at the top of their voices. Many of them were plainly tipsy. Augie kept his eyes on the rosy buff-colored girl at the head of the group. He had been made acquainted with her and learned that her name was Florence and that she was a church girl who lived with her aunt and was not considered fast. But Joe Baily and Tom Wright were still at her heels. They had little part in the merriment of the others. Their eyes were focused to a burning point. Both faces were avid, like the faces of starved dogs.

The crowd paused at a fresh-water spring on a level green spot. Several of the girls stooped to drink. Then the boys drank. As Tom Wright leaned above the water, Joe Baily gave him a little shove that ducked his face into the spring and wet the front of his shirt. Tom came up furious, humiliated in the presence of Florence. He got to his feet slowly and began fishing in the coat which he was carrying on his arm for his tool.

"I'm gonna shoot you, Joe Baily," he said.

"I'll be damned if you do, Tom Wright."

Joe whipped his own from his pocket and fired while Tom continued to fumble. The bullet went into the consumptive boy's belly. Still Tom kept fishing into the coat pocket. Joe banged again . . . then again.

"You betta keep shootin', Joe Baily, 'cause if ever I get ma hands on mine, I gonna kill you."

"You kilt Jimmy Hines, Tom Wright, but I'll be goddamned if ever you kills me." He banged two more into Tom's belly.

Tom dropped to his knees. As he fell, the pistol slid from his coat pocket to the ground. He reached forward feebly and picked it out of the grass.

"I'm gonna kill you, Joe Baily."

He fired once. Then his strength failed. But it was enough; the bullet whizzed through Joe's teeth. Joe pitched face forward. Tom curled into a knot, still holding his belly with one hand, and died in that position.

Nobody forgot that 'Mancipation Day picnic. It was the outing at which Joe Baily killed Tom Wright and Tom Wright killed Joe Baily. And the one from which Little Augie arrogantly rode home in a carriage with Florence, the yellow gal who was the real cause of the double murder.

IV

THE NEXT MORNING AUGIE AND BAD-FOOT Dixon sat in the barber shop, retelling the events of the picnic to a crowd of curious drifters and exchanging comments with them. Augie was enthroned in the first chair, having his hair trimmed, and Bad-foot, wearing an impressive checkerboard suit, was getting a manicure at the porcelain table.

Into the shop had come Mississippi Davis, a frock-tailed Negro hack-driver, Count Ragsdale, a gold-toothed gambler, and Barney Jones, a lazy young black, notorious for absurd fabrications.

"Sho I seen everything," Augie was boasting. "Tom Wright couldn't get to hisn 'cause it was stuck in his coat pocket. So Joe Baily banged down first. He shot dat lil raw-bony Tom Wright nuff times to kill a crocodile. But somehow or nuther he jes' couldn't drop him. Tom kept sayin', 'You shoot me, Joe Baily, but if ever I gets ma hands on mine, out goes yo' lamps.' "

"Joe Baily was one mo' bad nigger," Rags said. "All his people was bad niggers. Ma mammy tole me that his ole man, Luke Baily, kilt seben o' eight white mens to her knowings."

"Maybe he shot 'em, but he ain't kilt no white folks wid a six-shooter lak whut you kills niggers wid," Barney drawled. "Them six-shooters won't kill white folks."

"Hush dat, Bawney," Rags said. "Tha's a ignorant damn lie."

"De hell it is. I seen a nigger pistol a white man in Texas once. De white man got mad as a Tom-cat. 'Goddamn yo black mammy,' he says, 'is you shootin' me, nigger? Well, I'm gonna take a stick an' bus' yo' brains out for dat.' "

The barber shop crowd was used to Barney; they did not take his observations seriously. But they all knew that throughout the piney woods where Barney was brought up, there was any number of similarly depraved blacks who shared his awe of white folks. Barney was the city Negro's idea of a hayseed.

"Tom Wright was a bad young one, I thank you," Bad-foot said.

"Ah, *everybody* knows Tom Wright was bad," Rags said. "I seen him kill Jimmy Hines. Tom had de consumption, but dat ain't never stopped him from carrying his tool."

"He carried it for sumpin', too," Bad-foot said. "Tom sho would shoot, and you didn't have to beg him."

"Anybody'll shoot whut carries a gun," Barney said. "Hell, I seen a gun pop off layin' on a table."

"You is right, Barney," Augie laughed. "I can't tote no pistol on account o' dat. I'm right bad maself when I gets mad. Dat is, if I gets mad befo' I gets scairt. A pistol would jes' go off in ma hand without me pullin' de trigger."

Mississippi put on his battered silk topper and walked to the door. Suddenly he turned and said: "Niggers is crazy to shoot up one anuther dat-a-way. Dat's jes' whut white folks likes to see. Meantime they is doin'-up niggers right an' lef' an' nobody says boo."

"Tha's sumpin' whut you can't help," Augie said.

"Nah," Barney said. "You can't help whut de

white folks does to you. They is got things putty much they own way now. Out in Texas I seen a big black nigger hitched to a buggy lak a hoss. He was tied up beside de hitchin'-bar, drinkin' outa de tub. Directly a white lady come out o' de sto', got in de seat, an' switched his behin' wid a lil hoss whup, an' off he went trottin' down de street."

This amused Augie. "Wha, wha! If I'd 'a' been dat hoss, I'd 'a' run off wid dat buggy. Sho nuff; I'd 'a' run off jes' as sho as I's a nigger."

Mississippi ignored them. "Now dat yella gal, Florence Dessau. These niggers killing theyselfs about her, an' she ain't nuthin' but a white man's strumpet."

Augie flew out of the chair, the barber's mantle still around his neck.

"Whut dat you say, Mis'sippi?"

"Sho I said it. She ain't studyin' no niggers. She's a white man's gal, an' nobody knows it no better'n me."

"I's a mind to carve you for dat lie, Mis'-sippi," Augie said coldly. "Florence is a church gal. Her an' me is smitten. She is jes' sebenteen, an' her aunty looks after her. She ain't no chippie, Mis'sippi."

"I knows you is gettin' smitten on her, Lil Augie, but jes' keep yo' blade in yo' pocket, if you please. Sight beats de worl'. You come go wid me t'night."

"A'right," Augie said. "I'll go. But mind, it betta be de truf."

The barber shop became quiet. Augie and Badfoot went out, and promptly the rest of the crowd dispersed. Some clouds had blown in from the Gulf. It was going to rain.

At the appointed hour Augie met Mississippi. There was a heavy downpour that night, and the old hackman was sitting on the high driver's seat of his rig in a rubber raincoat. His miserable-looking horse was drenched. Augie, wearing a borrowed slicker, much too large for him, got to the seat beside Mississippi.

Under the street lamps the cobblestones glistened. Mississippi's lantern hollowed a small orange hole in the darkness; into it rain fell steadily. Now and again, above the hum of the downpour, there was the clank of an old iron gate. The drenched horse kept clogging along on the wet, resounding stones.

Finally they came to a stop, and sure enough,

a tall girl, waiting in the shadow of a doorway, rushed out and got into the trap. She did not speak. Mississippi turned his horse at the first corner. After a drive of fifteen or twenty minutes, he stopped again and the girl stepped quickly to the curbstone and ran up a flight of steps to a lighted door and touched a knocker. A white man came promptly and took her in his arms.

Augie saw that the man was young Horace Church-Woodbine, his own boss.

Augie felt no resentment, no bitterness toward Mississippi or Florence or Mr. Woody. But he was discouraged. He had set his mind on that fine girl. He liked tall yellow girls with painted mouths, and Florence was that exactly. He liked for them to dress well, and Florence wore finer clothes than any woman he had ever met. But what chance had he with a girl who was loved by Mr. Woody? All that shooting at the picnic had been wasted, it had done nothing to clear the picture so far as he was concerned. Thinking about it, Augie got the blues. Got them bad.

At home again, he took his new accordion from the box and began to play and sing.

GOD SENDS SUNDAY

If you don't b'lieve I love you
Look whut a fool I been.

"Go 'way, blues," he said aloud. "I'm borned lucky, an' I'm gonna have good luck right on. Go 'way, blues. My luck ain't change yet."

If you don't b'lieve I'm sinkin'
Look whut a hole I'm in.

The rain continued—invisible fingers against his panes, tiny unseen feet on the roof. "Go 'way, blues."

If you don't b'lieve I'm leavin'
Count de days I'm gone.

Augie decided to stop singing. But he did not stop playing. At intervals the music paused. During each interval, the silence said: "Go 'way, blues."

V

IN THE WEEKS THAT FOLLOWED, AUGIE learned something about Florence Dessau's past. As a small child, she had been given by her mother to an aunt. Later she was sent to the Catholic schools. But when she was twelve or thirteen, being tall and well developed, her aunt took her out so that she might work.

The aunt, Pheen, was a dressmaker, and Florence became one also. For two or three years they worked together on the satins and velvets of the fine women across town. Many of these women came to Pheen's house in luxurious carriages to call for their work or to leave orders. At other times, Pheen and Florence went into their handsome dwellings, taking fittings and consulting pattern catalogues.

Usually Florence served as Pheen's manikin

when they were engaged on one of the more exquisite gowns. She was of medium size, though above average height. Thus adorned, Florence was often so striking that Pheen would remark: "I mind you, young Miss St. Clare would give a heap for yo' shape when she gets in dat rag."

Even the wealthy women, seeing her standing in their unfinished frocks, would often exclaim suddenly, "What a lovely girl!" or "How well the child wears clothes!"

And these, no doubt, were the things that made Florence herself aware. Everywhere she went she saw men ogling her impolitely, both blacks and whites. Presently she became ashamed of her simple calico prints; she began to envy the gorgeous designs on which she and her aunt worked. By that time, too, she had seen how other attractive yellow girls had contrived to secure fineries. And so she pondered her thoughts.

One day, when she had been sent by Pheen to make a delivery at the home of some relatives of the Woodbines, Mr. Woody met her on the steps. The yellow girls had already whispered things about him from one to another. So Florence knew his reputation.

"Is that another one o' them pretty dresses in that box?"

"Hm. Yes, it's turribly putty, Mr. Woody."

"It's a Gawd's shame *you* ain't wearin' them pretty rags instead o' de ugly skates that live in there."

"Mis' Church is gonna look mighty fine in this here dress, Mr. Woody. You ain't gonna know her."

"She can't look lak you, yellow gal."

"Mr. Woody!"

"How would you lak a long velvet lak de one Miss Church wears, yellow gal?"

That was about a year before Augie met Florence at the picnic where Joe Baily and Tom Wright pistoled each other about her. In the months that followed he observed for himself Mr. Woody's interest in her. Florence became more and more striking. And Little Augie was near mad from coveting her. No other woman in New Orleans could please him. In the boogie places where he sometimes went with his cronies he slapped the teeth out of the strumpets who disgusted him and blacked their eyes. He earned the name of Little Poison.

Augie tried to make himself Florence's equal by wearing preposterous clothes. His pockets were still full of money. He had a suit for every day in the week and three for Sunday—bottle-greens, rust-browns, broad checked figures, light purplish blues; boxed coats, pinched backs, Prince Alberts. He loaded his fingers with rings and studded his ties with stickpins set with dazzling bloodstones.

But Florence steadily receded, further and further beyond his horizon. While he was following the races from one track to another, Mr. Woody was putting the girl in a handsome house of her own. He furnished it richly and provided a housekeeper. Later he gave her a carriage and a magnificent team of black horses and hired Mississippi as coachman.

In this queenly setting, Florence's beauty fascinated Augie more than ever. It seemed more unreal, more unattainable. He determined in his mind to talk to her once, at any rate, and tell her so, but even as he planned it he realized dimly that she was as far above his head as the moon. Yet he was unable to stay in his place; his arrogance kept coming up. So one morning he hired a carriage and drove by her house, ostensibly to pass a few words with Mississippi in the coach shed.

He did not leave the shed, however, until he saw Florence standing on her back steps. She came out into the sunshine to inspect a tiny spot on one of her dresses. Augie utterly misunderstood her motive.

"Howdy, Miss Florence."

"He-o, Lil Augie."

"Miss Florence, you is too putty an' yella to wash an' iron clo'es."

"Lawd, Lil Augie, I ain't never had ma hands in wash suds in all ma born days. I's jes' lookin' at dis ole dress to see if I ought to have it cleaned o' throw it away. I done wo' it five o' six times a'ready."

That pleased Augie. It fulfilled his idea of a truly fine woman.

"Oh! I didn't think so," he said. "I can putty nigh always tell a woman whut been bending over a wash tub too long. Hack hips, piano busts, an' skeeter legs. You is got shape, Miss Florence, an' it takes me to tell you so."

"You ain't makin' up to me, Lil Augie?"

"Yella gal, I loves you lak a hoss loves cawn, lak a fly do 'lasses. I loves you worser'n a hog loves to waller."

"You reckon Mr. Woody wants you to be lovin' me lak all dat?" She smiled pleasantly.

That took all the wind out of Augie's sails. He felt sure that his hopes were spoiled. But there was no need to spend the rest of his natural days mourning about it. He must think of something to do, something to occupy his mind. He could get a little peace by playing the accordion, and it helped somewhat to drink whiskey. But he could not stay drunk and be a good jockey. He could not carry the accordion every place he went, nor take it out and start playing every time he felt miserable. No, he would have to find something else. Maybe if he got another good-looking woman, that would help him to forget.

But he failed to find a suitable one in New Orleans; one of the jockeys told him, however, that there was a new world of fancy yellow women in St. Louis. So St. Louis became Augie's goal. He was going there within a few weeks to race, and at that time he proposed to explore.

Also, he had received word that his sister,

Leah, was now living there. He was anxious to see Leah again; he vainly imagined that he would be so happy he would dare to face his troubles, could he but spend a few more days under her roof.

"I'm no'thbound," he told his friends. "This heah town done shrunk up an' got too little for me. I done outgrowed it."

"Wha' you goin', Lil Augie? How long you gonna be gone?" they asked.

"I'm goin' to St. Louis," he said. "But I ain't sayin' how long."

VI

AUGIE WORE HIS FINEST THE DAY HE WENT
to look up his sister in St. Louis. He did not have
an exact address and had to make inquiries as he
walked along Wash Street. But he enjoyed the
stroll. It gave him an opportunity to strut himself
before the denizens of that neighborhood.

"I'm Lil Augie whut you reads about," he told
strangers. "I got a sister named Leah in dis end o'
town. Can you enlighten me?"

He was dressed in his favorite Prince Albert
with gray-striped pants and patent-leather shoes
beneath dove-colored spats. His silk topper
slanted rather unsteadily over his left eye, and
he carried a cane with a gold head. A celluloid
standing collar kept his chin in the air, and his
hands glistened with rich stones. Now and
again, as he strolled, he brushed the flaps of the

coat apart, disclosing an incredible flowered vest.

Filthy children, playing in the streets, came up to the sidewalk gaping with admiration. Augie flipped nickels and dimes at them and laughed as they scuffled in the dirt. He was smoking the long, expensive cigars that he most enjoyed, pausing frequently to light a fresh one, throwing the former aside with a majestic flourish.

That day the white sun beamed down on the dusty black neighborhood with the intense directness, the merciless concentration, of a burning-glass. The small brick houses of the Negroes seethed like ovens. From the open doors and windows wretched perspiring faces hung, faces as sad-eyed as owls. Women with thick hips, monstrous breasts, and glossy black skin stood on the doorsteps with brooms in their hands, their heads tied with red bandannas. The idle men folks, lean bucks with long feet and long, bony hands, with ugly razor scars on their faces, sat at the feet of the women, fanning.

Little Augie, following the foot-paths and exercising great care to protect his mirror-toed shoes from dust, had a vivid picture in his mind of the same streets during wet weather. There were no lilacs at these doorsteps such as he had been accustomed to seeing at doorsteps in Louisiana. But there was laughter none the less, loud-mouthed nigger laughter, and songs in the miserable stone houses.

When he finally located Leah's house Augie was greeted by a wild troop of strange mulatto children. From her kitchen window, Leah recognized him immediately, despite his unspeakable clothes and his gold teeth. For he had not grown an inch since the day he disappeared from the plantation. He was the same Little Augie. Leah stood for a second, blinded by the water that came into her eyes; her mouth dropped open, but she could not speak. Then suddenly something that had swollen up tight inside of her burst. Words poured out.

"Come! Looka heah! Ida! Lisha! Doll! Pig! Y'all chillun come heah quick. Tha's yo' Uncle Augie out there on de street. That lil bitta man in de fine clo'es."

It was then that Augie first saw the young savages tumbling from windows, flying down steps, coming toward him. He was almost frightened.

He had not been prepared to find Leah with a houseful of children, much less yellow ones.

"He-o, Uncle Augie."

"He-o, Uncle."

"He-o."

"He-o."

They tugged at his hands. He loved them immediately, but he drew back to make one reservation.

"Who done tole y'all I's yo' uncle?"

"Ah, you is Uncle Augie, a' right. Mamma seen you comin', she tole us."

"Well, lissen to me. I's gonna have to tell yo' mamma sumpin'. I ain't no 'uncle' to nobody. I is jes' plain Lil Augie. Y'all niggers is putty near big as me anyhow, an' talkin' 'bout 'uncle.' "

Of course, that won them. A fabulous relative who came dressed like a king and talking like that could do no wrong thereafter in their eyesight. By the time they had pulled him into the front room, Lisha had Augie's cane, swinging it above his head; Pig, the youngest, a ragged tot, had the silk hat over his ears; and the girls were swinging on the little man's arms.

Leah, a plain dark woman of medium size, old enough, apparently, for Augie's mother, came in and made a fuss over him. After the excitement, Augie pulled some green money from his pocket and sent the children to the store.

"Get 'bout half peck o' jaw-breakers an' stick candy," he said. "An' tell de man to send fo' o' five plugs o' Brown Mule chewin' bacca for Leah. Next time I come out heah I'm gonna bring y'all some presents whut's presents."

The youngsters filed out the door and up the street.

"Have some sit-down," Leah said.

Augie slid into his chair like a returned, embarrassed son and began telling Leah, quite simply but in great detail, the marvelous things that had happened to him since he left home. Due to the veil with which he had been born, his luck had been steadily good. All his friends had won good luck by being in his presence. Only one thing in life troubled him, he said. He was restless; he couldn't be satisfied long at a time, and he could not remain long in one place.

It was night when he finished the story. The

children were in their beds and asleep, and Augie and Leah were sitting on the front steps in the moonlight. Because of mosquitoes in the air, most of the houses on the street were unlighted, but the folks were still awake. In the darkness unseen hands plucked guitars. There were many voices, an assortment of nigger blues. Above them all, like their united echo, Augie heard a coarse voice crying, making a new song.

> *I hate to see de evenin' sun go down,*
> *Lawd, I hate to see de evenin' sun go down,*
> *'Cause de man I love done lef' dis town.*

Augie thought it was the best song he had ever heard.

"Lissen, Leah," he said, "whut dat?"

"Tha's a ole boogie-house song," she said scornfully.

"Lawd, Lawd!"

"You lak dat mess?"

"It's de most puttiest song that ever I heared," he said. "I gonna go home an' play it on ma 'cordion."

But he did not leave at once; another verse had begun.

GOD SENDS SUNDAY

Feelin' tomorrow lak I feel today,
Feelin' tomorrow jes' lak I feel today,
Gonna pack up ma trunk an' make ma
get-away.

When he finally returned to his room in the old Phoenix Hotel, Augie limbered up his instrument and repeated the tune from memory. Hearing the music, Bad-foot, who was lying across the bed asleep in his clothes, awoke and blinked. A couple of idle boys came in from adjoining rooms and listened. One of them knew some additional verses, verses intended for a man to sing.

A black-headed gal make a freight train
jump de track,
A black-headed gal make a freight train
jump de track,
But a long tall gal make a preacher ball
de jack.

A blond-headed woman make a good
man leave de town . . .

"Dat ain't no lie," Augie threw in.

"It ain't no sugar-mouth talk neither," Bad-foot said. "Them's ole hard-time facts."

> Lawd, a blond-headed woman make a good
>   man leave de town
> But a red-headed woman make a boy slap
>   his papa down.

The next evening Augie and Bad-foot, in company with their new friends, went out to inspect the fancy places on Targee Street and to make the acquaintance of some St. Louis sports. The St. Louis line was, in those days, celebrated from Omaha to Richmond; they earned for St. Louis the glowing reputation of capital of the Negro sporting wheel. Augie and Bad-foot had heard accounts of it from other race-horse men. In its bawdy establishments, according to these reports, the most elegant dusky harlots of the time sat for company . . . girls with stones like hen-eggs in their ears and teeth set with chipped diamonds.

That evening, in the summer twilight, the fancy brown girls swept down on the streets, as bright as flamingoes and as numerous. They had come out for a breath of air and a stroll before the evening's appointments. Going and coming through the blue evening, rather breathlessly on their high heels, twitching themselves and laughing, they struck Augie immediately with their charming insolence, their fierce hauteur and self-possession. He had never seen girls with such airs.

Walking down the procession of them, brushing their skirts as he passed, Augie was once more convinced that he had reached his dream. Here he could not fail to forget Florence Dessau, he could not fail to lose that restless feeling; here, he assured himself, he would be permanently happy. For here was a crowd of sports who met his own conception of fine living.

Many of the women had a love for gambling which Augie admired; many followed accounts of the horse races with interest; all had heard of Little Augie long before he came to their perfumed parlors on Targee Street. All the painted brown girls were partial to jockeys, for the horse-racing game in those days was one of the most lucrative fields open to ambitious young blacks. The fantastic renown won by jockeys was comparable to that of prize-fighters.

It was still too early for Augie's crowd to turn in to one of the establishments. The strollers were clustering together in small groups at street corners and on stoops. Augie and his friends came into the lighted entrance of a pool hall and propped themselves on their canes. A little later they went in.

Some one introduced Augie to the sparkling proprietor. This was obviously a hang-out for macks, the sweet men of the period. A crowd of gaudy coatless young fellows surrounded the tables, bowing over cues. They wore gay embroidered shirts, and on their fingers, below the knuckle-length sleeves, flashed diamonds and polished nails. Their finery seemed even to exceed that of the fancy women who supported them. Gold money made into jewelry was customary, also high-roller hats, like Augie's, with nude women or boxers or racing-horses worked in small eyelets in the crown. Several of the sports, hearing Augie's name, drew near to shake his hand and be introduced.

Augie eyed them with unbounded pleasure. He kept saying to himself, "This heah is ma company. These niggers is fancy; they is ma kind."

A few hours later, in one of the cologne- and musk-scented places, Augie met Della Green. She was waiting in a small front room overcrowded with old-fashioned horsehair furniture. A large lamp with a painted shade furnished a dim light. Two other girls were in the room, quietly smoking cigarettes; still others were moving about in the large adjoining room. Bad-foot and the others went in there to drink, but Augie sat rapt, his eyes fixed on Della. She wore magenta cloth, and her hair was short and brushed in pompadour fashion; it was curly brown hair, the hair of a mulatto, and her skin was buff. There were a few freckles on her nose and an artificial beauty spot near the left eye.

Augie walked across the room nervously and sat beside her on the couch. She met him smiling, but somehow he found it hard to approach her, hard to begin talking. His eyes were round and childlike.

"Do you want to be alone wid me, Lil Augie?"

His thoughts seemed to return from a long way. "Oh, yes. Tha's it; le's you an' me get together."

Actually, he was in no hurry. He did not merely want to go upstairs with Della. It had occurred to him that this was the kind of girl he would like to possess, to exhibit on the streets, to boast of to his cronies.

A scrawny black girl with a hideous mouth brought in a small lighted lamp. Holding this above her head, Della led Augie up a dim stairway. The unlovely black girl followed directly and placed a bottle and two whiskey glasses on a bed stand.

With Augie, Della refrained from the customary tricks of her profession. She must have felt that he was in no mood to have his head rubbed, that it would not arouse him. Instead she kept filling his glass. At length his eyes brightened; he began to feel once more like a big man who could manage women in his own way.

"Don't I suit you, Lil Augie? You look at me so funny."

"You is good for ma eyes, gal. Tha's how come I looks at you."

"Sho nuff?"

"I been lookin' all over de country for you."

"Ah, Lil Augie! You is tryin' to swell ma haid."

"Swell nuthin'. I been lookin' for jes' sich a gal as you."

"They tells me yo pockets is loaded wid spikes, Lil Augie."

"Sho, I's dirty wid money, an' I don't mind spendin' it."

"You is sweet to pick out a ole ugly gal lak me, Lil Augie."

Augie stretched across the bed in a ridiculous oversized nightshirt. By now he was too exhilarated to mind his appearance. He crossed his legs triumphantly and lit a cigar. Della drew a crimson kimono over her ruffled nightdress.

"Whose box is dat in de corner?" Augie asked.

"It's mine. You lak music, Lil Augie?"

"Jes' crazy 'bout it," he said. "I plays de 'cordion maself. Pick me sumpin' on de box."

Della sat at the foot of the bed, facing Augie, her feet curled beneath her. She began strumming chords; later she sang a medley of songs for Augie, songs old and familiar to the places on Targee Street. She had a soft weeping voice, well suited to her songs and to Augie's taste.

Gwine to de river, take a rockin'-chair,
Gwine to de river, take a rockin'-chair,

Arna Bontemps

If de blues overtake me gwine rock away
from dere.

Augie's spirits continued to rise. His eyes kept feasting on Della's fine small body, her smiling girl-face.

If I could holler lak a mountain jack,
If I could holler lak a mountain jack,
I'd go up on de hillside an' call ma rider back.

She changed the chords, and Augie contributed a stanza of another tune.

If de river was whiskey an' I was a duck
I'd dive to de bottom an' never come up.

Della answered:

Silk stockings an' ruffled drawers
Got many a po' man wearin' overalls.

"Turn down de lamp now," Augie said, "an' put de box back in de corner."

"A' right, Lil Augie. Mus' I send word to yo' friends?—de ones whut come in wid you?"

"Oh, yea. Tell 'em to go 'bout they business, 'cause I ain't studyin' 'bout 'em no mo' this night."

Della laughed. She called the plug-ugly girl to the door.

"Tell de bad-foot gentaman an' his frien's not to wait for Lil Augie," she said.

VII

DESPITE THE BRILLIANT RISE OF HIS FOR-
tunes, his enormous success on the sporting
wheel, Little Augie had a rival in Targee Street. He
had to contend with Biglow Brown, a magnificent ginger-colored giant, for the spotlight.

What Biglow lacked of Augie's glamour, his
superior physical charms supplied. He was six
feet three and had large, fine hands and a savage
bearing that was the rage of the fancy-houses.
Since coming to St. Louis a few years earlier, he
had enjoyed a lurid popularity along the line, a
sort of renown that Augie could never hope to
duplicate. For Biglow was precisely everything
that Little Augie was not. He succeeded without
money or the glowing aid of a legend. On the
other hand, he was entertaining; he was a loud,

sassy talker, and his extraordinary body was a feast for the gaze of the women.

Biglow had come to St. Louis from Georgia with a Negro minstrel show. In the few days the troop remained, he prospered so well that he decided to remain and desert his company. The possibilities for a first-water maquereau on Targee Street struck him as infinitely finer than his prospects on the stage and more to his taste. He was promptly taken in by one of the veteran trollops, decorated in the gaudy manner, and put on display.

Being young, however, and unacquainted with the requirements of his position, Biglow soon got himself into difficulties. While his woman was busy with her appointments he made passes at other girls, and he was unwise enough to boast of his duplicity. The quick result of his proud words was a fight.

The two women met in an alley, unknown to Biglow, and shouted accusations at each other. A yellow light fell upon their shoulders from an uncurtained upper window. The young rival of Biglow's middle-aged woman was a dark girl with Indian-like features and straight hair. Suddenly they hurled themselves together like mad cats. The older woman's hair became bushed on her head, and her clothes were promptly hanging from her body in rags; the younger one fought in a crouch, her shoulders rounded and her head lowered. Now and again they broke their holds, separated, then flew back again with increased venom. Presently they fastened themselves to each other so bitterly their united bodies reeled and dropped to the ground, the younger woman's teeth in the older one's cheek, the older one gouging at her opponent's eyes.

Both of them lost Biglow. For a middle-aged strumpet with a nasty scar on her face could offer little to a fastidious young mack. And little more could be expected from the fortunes of a black gal with one eye. He went directly to an elegant slim girl named Lila who was employed at the time in one of the houses that served a white clientele. He did not get along with Lila either, not smoothly at any rate, but he had profited by his earlier experience. He had learned to keep certain things from the gossipers, and he had found a way of strengthening his position by the use of violence.

The macks knew that the nature of women

requires a certain modicum of brutality; and experience had shown that unless they received it at the hands of their lovers occasionally they would turn and lump one another. But this latter was a bad thing. It was a man's duty.

So Biglow, with his great physical power, became a sweet terror to his woman and to those with whom he jibed. If they said anything that did not please him, he slapped them with his open hand; if they accused him of infidelity, he roared like a caged panther, broke whatever he touched, and finally hurled the lamp at them and stomped out of the room.

When Little Augie came to town, Biglow was still on Lila's string, but he had been playing around with Della. For Della's star was just rising; she was comparatively a novice and had as yet no regular mack relying on her support. Soon after Augie's arrival Biglow quarreled with Della and blacked both her eyes. Augie knew Biglow by that time, and when Della told him of the skirmish he became heated.

"I ain't gonna have it. No nigger is gonna lump yo' eyes lak dat, long as I's in town. I feels ma love comin' down, an' I can't stan' it."

"Ah, don't worry yo' mind, Lil Augie, ma eyes'll be a' right soon."

"From now on I'm gonna be de one to give you yo' knocks when you needs 'em. On'erstand?"

"That suits me," she giggled.

"You can tell that Biglow Brown that after today he got to come by me. Put his hands on you one mo' time, an' me an' him is gonna have it."

"That is mighty proud talk for such a lil man," she said.

Augie jumped to his feet, bouncing nervously. "Yea? Well, I might be lil but I's loud as a six-gun. An' I wants anybody whut don't think so to try me a barrel. Tell that nigger I said so."

Augie banged the door and went downstairs, stomping his heels to emphasize his words. On the street, in the quiet light, he felt as tall and formidable as his own tremendous shadow. But soon his love started to coming down again, and his pride melted. He began thinking of things to buy for Della to show his feeling. To begin with, he would take her out of the sporting place and set her up in a house of her own—like Mr. Woody had done for Florence. Then he would buy her clothes like the ones Florence wore. He wanted her to be as nearly like Florence as possible.

In his room, Augie talked his plans to Badfoot. The older man by now approved of everything Augie did or said. With these new proposals, as with all the other suggestions of Augie, he was immensely pleased. Della was one of the youngest and best-looking fancy girls on Targee Street (which was saying much), and Little Augie was well able to keep her in the gaudy fashion to which she had become accustomed.

The next day was Saturday, and Augie returned from the race track as jubilant as a schoolboy. He had enjoyed the best day of his entire experience with horses. He had ridden three winners, and the excited spectators had thrown him more than three hatfuls of greenbacks, not to mention small change and cigars, to express their pleasure in him. All this, on the heels of his plans for Della, in addition to his formal earnings, intoxicated him. He knew, furthermore, that in the next day's papers his name would appear in big letters. Everybody would be talking about Little Augie.

He hurried to his room, changed to a fresh

suit of clothes, a fresh candy-striped shirt, and a flowered vest. Then he went out to the barber shop for finishing touches. He was so exhilarated he forgot to eat supper, but hired a pretentious two-horse rig with a frock-tailed driver and went directly from the shop to Della's place.

Della came down to meet him in voluminous ruffled silks, a wine-colored dress under which yellow petticoats peeped. Her mouth was red, and she was hatless, her short hair neatly brushed and odorous with pomade. She was more resplendent than Augie had yet seen her. In the moonlight she seemed, to Augie, irreproachable; not a fault was visible. Augie felt like a man who sells toy balloons at a fair when suddenly, loosing the strings he is holding, he sees above his head the sky full of the bright lovely things, gradually ascending on the wind.

"Bring de box 'long," he called to Della. "Us gonna ride in de pawk an' out 'cross de country. We gotta have some tunes."

"An' sweeten' water, too, Lil Augie. You mus' get us some rock-candy an' gin to make sweeten' water."

"Da's de ticket, baby. Mus' have out lil sweeten' water."

At the first saloon Augie ordered the rig to stop and dispatched the hackman to get a pint of gin and to take a drink himself while at the bar. When he returned Augie tossed off about an inch of the liquor and dropped the candy into the bottle. Della tasted it.

"Let it set a lil while," she said.

Augie pressed the cork and slipped the bottle into his pocket.

The hackman drove them beyond the bawdy section, beyond the squalid homes of the poor Negroes and across the city. The night seemed cool in the open-topped carriage. There were trees on Enright Street and overhead a few large stars that throbbed insecurely in their places and seemed about to fall. Augie was speechless with pleasure.

"Whut de matter, Lil Augie? Cat got yo' tongue?"

"I's jes' studyin', baby."

"Has you got troubles, Lil Augie?"

"Troubles? Gal, I's as free of troubles as de

palms of ma hands is free from hair. I's ridin' on de moon."

"You is lucky."

"Oh, I was borned lucky. I's borned wid a veil. Tha's sho nuff lucky."

"Sho, a veil is lucky."

"Anybody whut takes up wid me gets lucky, too," he said. "Look at Bad-foot. I made him lucky. I gonna make you lucky too if you loves me hard enough."

"I gonna love you hard, Lil Augie. I gonna love you worser'n ever I did love ara other man."

"You gonna love me worser'n you do Biglow?"

"Shucks. That nigger ain't in it. Not de way I gonna love you."

"Yea? Tha's good. But dis gonna be de law: You can stay in de business a lil longer an' sit for de company an' all dat, but nara other man can beat you. Jes' me. I gonna be de one to give you yo' knocks. I means it, an' I don't want no two-timin'. Nobody beats you but me. On'erstand?"

"Sho, Lil Augie. I done promise you dat."

"A'right. I jes' want us to have things plain."

Their carriage had reached the park and was moving slowly on the hilly dirt roads. Augie's diamonds flashed like fireflies in the darkness. He kept lighting fresh cigars. Della, beside him, her head tossed back, began picking the guitar. Augie thought of the bottle. He shook it before drawing the cork, and they both took long drinks. Then he lit a cigarette for Della and put it in her mouth. She didn't stop picking. Augie sang:

> I got a belly full o' whiskey an' a head
>   full o' gin;
> De doctors say it'll kill me but they don't
>   say when.

Della sang back:

> See, pretty papa, pretty papa, look whut
>   you done done,
> You made yo' mamma love you, now yo'
>   woman's come.

"Ah, you sassy wench!"

Both of them drank more sweetened water. Presently the moon whitened the park, and the tipsy Negroes, singing in their carriage, began to attract the attention of other drivers on the quiet road. But they did not worry. They finished the bottle and tossed it in the road. The rig came out of the park and on to a country drive. Augie had become mellow and amorous.

The frock-tailed hackman stopped to rest his horses a moment beside a creek. In his high seat, with the mashed-up silk topper on one side of his head, he looked as grotesque as a scarecrow.

Augie sought his girl's mouth. He could hear her breath, he could feel the heaving of her breast. Upon her face he saw the lace shadows of overhanging tree leaves.

"Is y'all ready to start home?" the hackman asked.

"Yea, I guess we betta start," Della said.

"Sho," Augie said. "Le's get goin'."

The next day was quiet for Augie. Being Sunday, he was not required to go to the race track. Targee Street was dull too. The sporting folks, having put in a heavy night, slept late in anticipation of another big one to come. The macks were lolling on the streets in their petticoat-silk shirts—that is, they wore vests without coats, the vests hanging open, the embroidered figures and candy-stripes in full display. Augie, however, never lolled like this. He wore a Prince Albert on Sunday mornings and carried a cane. And he did not lean against store fronts or gate posts. He felt himself obliged to maintain a certain dignity in Sunday clothes, to stand erect and to keep moving whenever possible.

"Hot damn!" his admirers greeted him.

"No flies is on Lil Augie."

"No, suh, Lil Augie is got de worl' tee-rolled."

"Three winners in one day! Three hats full o' money!"

"Lil Augie is got de worl' tee-rolled."

In the afternoon, Augie took Bad-foot over to Leah's house on Wash Street. He was anxious to make his old friend acquainted with his sister, and furthermore, he needed Bad-foot to help him with the packages of presents he had bought for Leah's children. When they arrived, the youngsters had just returned from Sunday school and were sitting around a small kitchen table with improvised bibs tucked under their chins to keep their Sunday-go-to-meeting clothes unspotted. Leah was standing over them with an iron kettle of mustard greens cooked with ham hocks, replenishing their plates directly from the pot.

After the meal the children stormed the front room and Augie opened his packages . . . suits of blue two-pocket overalls trimmed with red, brass-toed shoes, rubber bands to make "nigger-shooters"; Topsy dolls for the girls, and a tiny suit of man's clothes for little Pig. When the gifts were properly apportioned, Leah put them away and sent the children to play. Later she cut a cool watermelon, and she, Augie, and Bad-foot sat on the front steps eating generous slices.

Augie stayed until evening; then he began to feel restless. So he left the two older people quietly smoking their pipes and rocking on Leah's stoop and hurried over to Targee Street. But it was useless. Della was occupied with company, and he had to wait to see her. This gave him an opportunity to think and fret. It occurred to him that he needed but one thing to insure his happiness, to make it complete. He needed Della for himself; that would forestall such disappointments in the future. Yes, that was the thing, and he would arrange it immediately. This would be her last Sunday night with the company. His love was coming down.

And within a week he made good his intentions. Della was moved into a brick house with furnishings like Florence's house in New Orleans. She was dressed in cloth exactly like that worn by Florence. And she looked for all the world like Florence, except that she was smaller. But she was not Florence.

Meanwhile Augie's luck continued at the race track. He had, since coming to St. Louis, won a place among the first-rank jockeys, and Mr. Woody was talking about sending him to New York and Maryland to ride for the rich purses being offered on those tracks. Meanwhile, too, the St. Louis season was drawing to a close. There were but a few more days. Then, Augie would have to go with his stable to Louisville, to Mobile, and finally back again to New Orleans.

During those remaining days, however, there was to be the Cotton Flower Ball, the fête of the year for the black sports and fancy women of St. Louis. It was an event celebrated wherever there were fast Negroes and attended by folks from

Kansas City, Omaha, Memphis, and New Orleans as well as the St. Louis crowd. The Cotton Flower cakewalk was in the nature of an intersectional competition. In none of the other cities was there a festival to match it, a festival with its tradition and reputation for splendor.

Augie had heard about the Cotton Flower Ball for years. So he looked forward to attending his first one with more than ordinary interest. For he did not intend to be a cipher in the great mass of people who would throng Stokes Hall that evening. He determined to make himself attractive so that he would be noticed, so that he would reflect his real importance. He determined to dress Della in such clothes as would become the woman of Little Augie.

Through the intervening days, these preparations occupied his thought continuously. All his spare hours were spent in the more tawdry tailoring establishments, consulting catalogues and examining cloth. In these places he encountered other dandies, equally determined to make a vivid impression. Augie did not underestimate his rivals; he had been in St. Louis long enough to know what the sartorial competition one had to meet there was like.

The high spot of the Ball would, of course, be the cakewalk. And in cakewalks, clothes were always a factor in the rivalry. Augie wrung his hands and walked the floor like a man in agony. But when the night of the Ball came, he was ready. Gloriously ready.

VIII

CROWDS BEGAN TO ASSEMBLE EARLY ON the corner of Thirteenth and Biddle Streets. Little temporary booths were opened beneath the street light, along the sidewalk. An elderly Negro in a white cap and a white apron was loudly announcing craw-daddies from a tiny stand. As he called to passers he himself kept eating in order to entice their appetites. A sweet-potato man with a small tin oven fastened to the frame of an old go-cart walked back and forth past the entrance of the Hall. In the crude little booths sliced watermelon, corn on the cob, soda pop, and red stick candy were on display. Each booth had a small bell with which to arrest attention, but bells were unnecessary, for the busy black proprietors were already hard-pressed and perspiring.

These early crowds were composed largely of drifters, folks who had come to stand apart and catch glimpses of the doings without participating, people unable to pay the fabulous entrance fee of four bits or to wear the clothes that such fêtes demanded. They were made up of unclean children, shabby adolescent boys, fat handkerchief-headed mammies, and feeble old men. All of them kept crowding toward the entrance while a uniformed attendant pushed and hauled those who came too near, and threatened to cuff the ones who didn't like it.

About nine-thirty the first carriages drove up and the guests commenced to arrive. Once started, the stream of arrivals was steady. Every available rig in that end of town was pressed into use.

The cakewalk began at eleven. The leader gave a signal; the fiddles took their cue; banjos, guitars, bull fiddles, and mandolins responded graciously, and the large hall resounded. There were bright paper hangings from the ceiling, gay decorations on the walls, flags and banners, and a transparent waxed floor beneath the suspended lamps.

Arna Bontemps

After a few preliminary bars of music, the first steppers emerged from a side room. The crowd across the hall, in a roped-off area, applauded noisily. A tall chocolate boy in a sky-blue suit with large white buttons was walking with a girl in yellow. With every step the tall boy twirled his cane and cut a brief pigeonwing. The girl followed his lead, her arm in his, her skirt caught in one hand and raised mischievously.

This couple set an extremely high requirement for the walkers who were to come. But the gay procession that followed did not disappoint the spectators. Each new couple presented a new conception of color, an individuality of step, and each was greeted by a fresh burst of applause. Wide silk skirts were tossed in the air, disclosing flame-bright petticoats. It continued, endlessly it seemed, adding color to color, brightness to brightness, till the dance floor was a gaudy whirling pin-wheel. The men, as in all primitive groups, were the most elegant.

With so many impressive pairs on the floor, it became apparent that selecting a winner was to be no simple task. The room buzzed with amazed exclamations. Here and there, small groups argued the merits of their favorites. Suddenly the buzzing ceased. There was a hush, then a burst of cheers and furious applause. It was so wild and sudden that all arguments ended. Every head was turned, every neck strained. Little Augie had taken the floor with Della Green.

He wore a full dress suit made of leaf-green satin, with a cape and top hat to match. His lapels were gold, as were also his pumps and the knob of his green cane, and his hair was oiled and pressed to his head like patent leather. Della's dress was plum-colored, her petticoats gold; she too wore gold slippers. Their walk was simply an elaborate strut, but it was effective enough.

"Tha's it," the crowd shouted. "Tha's de one."

"Yes, suh. Lil Augie takes de cake."

"Lil Augie is *it*. There ain't no flies on him."

"Yes, suh. Lil Augie takes de cake."

The walk was promptly decided; there was no longer a doubt anyway. With that feature of the evening over, a wan ebony fellow took his place in the front of the instruments and called the steppers to get ready to dance. He was going to call figures. But Augie was not interested in this, it was like an anticlimax to him; his success had already been complete. He withdrew to the sidelines and allowed Della to dance with one of the young macks who had been pestering her.

Della was more devoted to dancing than was Augie. He watched her as she made the routine steps, her head tossing proudly, and he marveled again and again at her striking resemblance to Florence. But she was not Florence. He knew that, and the thought saddened him, in the midst of all this giddy crowd and in the wake of his own spectacular triumph.

During a respite, while the dancing partners shifted, Augie saw Biglow coming insolently down the floor in a buff-colored suit and a crimson vest. His hair was parted in the middle, and he was unquestionably handsome. But Augie thought he discerned a simpering air about the big fellow, like the air of a woman. Despite Biglow's unusually magnificent body, he had that offensive softness characteristic of all the macks, a softness which Little Augie, despite his inferior size, curiously lacked.

Biglow reached Della, and they danced. Later he followed her off the floor, and Augie heard him speaking to her.

"You know right well whut kind o' mack I is. Any woman dat messes wid me gotta take de lumps. I'd slap yo' eyeteeth out, an' I don't care when or where."

Augie stepped up. "Lissen a minute, Mistah Biglow Brown. Lil Augie can whup his own womens. An' there ain't no mack in St. Louis gonna do ma job. Lil Augie is loud as a six-gun."

Biglow looked down on Augie as on a child. "Lil Augie, if ever I got real mad I'd put a lil bitta man lak you in ma coat pocket an' go on 'bout ma business."

"I done said mine. If you or any other mack don't think so, jes' try me a barrel."

"Hm. Puh."

"Jes' 'hm' an' 'puh' all you is a mind to. If you don't think so, try me a barrel."

"Tha's big-man talk, son."

"Sho it's man talk. I ain't fattenin' meat for some other nigger to slice."

"You betta keep yo' chippie at home den."

"I ain't gonna keep her at home neither."

"You is beggin' trouble, Lil Augie."

"Not heah, Biglow Brown. Not t'night."

IX

RELATIONS BETWEEN AUGIE AND BIGLOW became increasingly strained during the days that followed. Biglow was scarce on Targee Street, and that inspired the rumors that he was ducking Augie, rumors that Augie had threatened to call his hand the first time they met and to make the big fellow back water. These were probably false, for Augie too was scarce along the line and was plainly not seeking trouble. But when the tales reached Biglow he became at once furious and defiant. No little imitation man like Augie was going to make a show of him, he told folks. The fact that Augie was famous in sporting circles and that his pockets were loaded with gold spikes meant nothing to Biglow Brown. And as for Della, he was sure that she would gladly leave Augie's cage and go back to work if she had the inducement of a maquereau like himself. In Biglow's opinion, the nigger who could match his speed with women had not yet shown himself in St. Louis.

Finally, to prove that he was as bold as he pretended, as scornful of Little Augie, he called to see Della in her new home. That evening Augie had gone out with Bad-foot to refresh himself and to risk a few dollars on the bones. He had left Della sitting with her guitar at the low window of their front room, smoking. She was still there, an hour later, when Biglow came around the corner.

"He-o, Della," he said.

"He-o, Biglow. Whut's on yo' mind?"

"Liquor an' womens, baby."

"That's all?"

"Hm. Them's all I study 'bout."

"Well, whut you doin' over in dis end o' town den?"

"Driftin'. Thought I'd stop in an' chew de rag wid you."

She lit a fresh cigarette and began twanging at the box. After a moment Biglow said: "Ain't you gonna ask me to come in an' have some sit-down?"

"Nah, you can't come in heah, Biglow."

"How come dat? Whut's done got 'tween me an' you?"

"Nuthin', Biglow. I jes' don't want no trouble."

"Wha', wha'! You mean Lil Augie?"

"He ain't got nuthin' for you to do."

"He scairt I'll get his gal, hunh! I thought he was sich a big-timer. He tries to make out lak nobody in de worl' can't tee-roll him. Wha', wha'! Well, he betta mind how he leaves you sittin' heah in de window by yo'self, 'cause Papa Biglow is first one place, then anuther."

Biglow shoved his hat back, leaning with one hand on the sill. Della's house was dark, but the light of a street lamp brightened the window and the front room. Under its yellow illumination, the broad stripes of Biglow's pretentious suit showed vividly.

When Augie returned, Biglow was still standing in that position, still trying to talk his way into the house. Augie walked past the big Negro without speaking. In the house he whispered to Della: "Shut de window, baby."

Biglow remained for a moment outside the closed window without moving; then he grinned, pulled his hat down over his right eye, and slowly shambled away.

The next evening, when Augie returned from the track, he found Della lying across the bed, her clothes stripped to ribbons and her face badly bruised. For a moment Augie lost his mind; he became so furious he could not speak. His voice choked, and water came into his eyes. Biglow had defied him. It was as plain as day. After the little gesture of the previous night, the big mack had returned and given Della a beating, the one thing that Little Augie could not endure. If he had been intimate with her in some other way, it would not have been as bad. But this invaded the one province that Augie believed to be his own. And it was done for pure spite. Little Augie's mind left him again.

He hastily found his tool and hurried across to Targee Street and began asking the people he met if any of them had seen Biglow. At length he located him in the macks' pool hall, but it then occurred to Augie that the hour was a bit early for a blow-off; there were too many people about. So he decided to keep his eye on his man and await his time. He strolled calmly up and down the block, his eyes fixed on the poolroom entrance. Several times he went into a saloon and drank. While he delayed he was assailed by fears, but he kept putting them out of his mind. About eleven-thirty he sent a message into the poolroom for Biglow by a small boy. Then he quickly stepped around the corner and waited at the head of an alley.

Biglow seemed a long time coming, and Augie became aware of his own trembling. Suddenly he noticed a woman in the alley. She was standing in the glow of an upper window, and Augie saw that her black face had features like an Indian and that she had straight Indian-like hair; one eye was out. After a moment she walked past Augie and stood in the light of the street.

Then Biglow came around the corner, a small pearl-handled pistol in his hand. He confronted the woman a moment in silence. The sight of her seemed to disgust him.

"You! Well, I'll be goddamned!"

He slapped her to the ground with his left hand. Augie leapt from the shadow that contained him. In the same instant his six-gun barked. Root-a-toot-toot . . . toot-toot.

The woman was still sobbing on the dusty ground. Augie vaguely felt a crowd gathering at the head of the alley, in the light of the street. He stood like a clay man, unable to move, holding the same attitude in which he had shot Biglow. Everything became unreal. When he came out of his dream the police were hauling him, with the woman, into their wagon.

Augie was out of jail in time for Biglow's funeral. In those days red-light murders were so commonplace they evoked but slight interest from the court authorities. Condemnations were rare. Almost anything passed for self-defense. Consequently the impression got about that the state did not wish to bother with crimes committed by Negroes against Negroes.

The whole affair continued dreamlike to Augie. He did not fully awaken until he left the Four Court Jail two days later, a free man. There remained in his memory only disconnected fragments of the spectacle, a spectacle in which he seemed hardly to have been concerned. There had been a great deal of churchlike ceremony, a lot of mumbling that sounded like prayer, a procession of ghostly robed figures, and a tendency on the part of attendants to draw the Bible on every one who entered the courtroom. He had a dim picture of Mr. Woody suavely telling the judge that the little fellow was his nigger, a fine well-behaved sort and an excellent jockey. Leah, Bad-foot, and the Indian-looking woman all appeared briefly as in a mist, said a few words, and departed. It was hard to imagine the woman's attitude, since she had lost an eye in a fight about this same murdered mack a few years earlier. But at this time she said nothing damaging to the defendant.

In the end, the judge complimented Little Augie for his reputation as a jockey and advised him to avoid the company of bad niggers like Biglow in the future. For, he said, it would be a shame to have such a bright career on the race track cut short. So with Bad-foot and Leah, Augie walked out into the morning sunshine and into the literal world again.

Della was waiting for him anxiously. When Augie saw her face that day, it was like a revelation. He knew positively that she loved him hard.

She was sitting at her window strumming the box, but she looked wasted, as if she had been worried and had failed to eat regularly. Her eyes were swollen.

"Lil Augie!" she exclaimed.

"Bring it to me," he commanded. "Lemme taste dat sugar."

He kissed her soft painted mouth. "I tell you 'bout me," he said. "Lil Augie is too bad. I borned lucky. I gonna make you lucky too."

"I believe dat, Lil Augie."

"Did you love me hard when I was in de lock-up?"

"Too hard. I been lovin' you worser'n a schoolboy loves pie."

"Hm. Tha's good."

That afternoon Augie was not slated to ride; so he did not go to the track. Instead he hired a carriage and took Della to Biglow's funeral. He had not been anxious to attend; he did not like to be reminded of death, for one thing, and in this case there was a special horror attached to the body of Biglow. But Della persuaded him that it was the conventional thing to do. It would show that he held no rancor against the man he had shot, that the thing was really done in self-defense. Another reason was that *everybody* was going to be present, all the fancy set, and there was bound to be some fine moaning.

Augie dressed modestly in a salt-and-pepper suit, and Della wore a veil. They took inconspicuous seats in the funeral parlor and lowered their heads respectfully. To Augie the large room, sweetened by the odors of the floral pieces, was all but intolerable. A profusion of songs filled his mind, sad and hurtful songs that only extremely happy people dare to sing. . . . Blues are unbearable to a person who is really distressed. For that reason, Augie supposed the preacher on the platform had raised the happy lyric, "Yes, We'll Gather at the River."

The crowd finished assembling. The room was packed with fancy women, macks, and gamblers. About a hundred others, Negroes of the same stamp, were outside, jostling roughly to gain a peep through the door. Most of the macks were in black, but under the dark suits they had on the gayly embroidered candy-striped shirts characteristic of their profession. Most of them were

extremely young boys, quickly and unwhole-
somely matured, and all had the same wan lap-
dog expression on their too smooth faces.

The sermon and the eulogy were brief, as
they had to be if they were to avoid a hint of
the ridiculous; and the chief feature of the
funeral was the parade to view the remains. One
by one the macks paused before the open casket,
drew from their pockets immense petticoat-silk
handkerchiefs, buried their faces, and staggered
away. It was terribly sincere. The veiled strumpets screamed. At each scream Augie shuddered.
It was not like church folks wailing to heaven.

"This heah is one mo' sad funeral," Augie told
himself. "De preacher done shet his book an' all
dat, but dis funeral is jes' nachally too sad. Oo-
wee! I can't hardly stand it. I wish I was a lil ole
baby on dat doggone plantation again, wid Leah
an' all 'em. Oo-wee!"

In the procession of carriages going out to St.
Peter's cemetery, Augie leaned back beside Della
and sang in his mind:

> Look down, look down dat lonesome road
> Befo' you travels on.

Arna Bontemps

At the graveyard he sang:

Ashes to ashes an' dust goes back to dust,
Said, ashes to ashes, dust goes back to dust.

The others (the macks, the trollops, the gamblers, and their followers) were singing audibly, "We Shall Meet to Part, No, Never."
But it was not like church niggers singing.

Augie's days in St. Louis had come to an end. In twenty-four hours he would be on his journey. He looked forward to the many races he would ride on Churchill Downs, to those in Mobile and New Orleans, and to the vague uncertain ones in New York and Maryland. But it was not so much the actual racing he craved as the unbroken companionship of the horses. Life as he had experienced it in St. Louis was much too complicated for his taste. It was like trying to puzzle out a combination lock. Augie was not sorry to get away. Only a few weeks before, he had been sure that at last he had found his place, the place where he could lose that restless feeling and become permanently happy. Now here he was, at the end of the racing season, aching to get away.

Before leaving he made another visit to Leah's house and left a roll of paper money with her. Leah wanted to go farther west with her children, and Augie decided to give her money to go on. Leah's house would always be his real home, and he did not want to be required to recall St. Louis and Biglow every time he thought of her. St. Louis was haunted for Augie. With his supernatural sight, he might expect to see Biglow's ghost on Targee Street almost any night.

Leah cried on his shoulder. "I jes' hopes for one thing," she said. "I hopes to see you get a good quiet gal an' settle down. I hopes to see you quit them race hosses an' all de gamblers an' get a steady job."

"I'm a race-hoss man, Leah," he said tenderly. "You know whut becomes of ducks when they don't get to de water? Well. That's me to a T."

That night Augie stayed at home with Della. She played the box, and they sat together on a little old-fashioned couch. Augie put a bottle of gin and rock candy, sweetened water, within reach. It occurred to him, when the bottle was nearly empty, that he had never given Della a beating. That was a serious neglect. A beating was an act of singular intimacy between a gal and her man. Della had been good to him, and there was no reason why he should leave her in doubt of his passion. He took another drink and decided to attend to that item at once.

"I got one mo' bone to pick wid you, baby," he said.

"Whut dat, Lil Augie?"

" 'Bout Biglow. You ain't never give account o' whut he was doin' round heah so many times."

"He jes' come, Lil Augie. I ain't ask him. I loved you too hard."

"Maybe that so an' maybe it ain't. But I'm gonna beat you 'bout it anyhow."

He quickly boxed both her cheeks.

"You hurt me, Lil Augie."

"I means to hurt," he said. "I wants you to know I think a heap o' you an' I ain't gonna fail to give you de lumps you deserve. Lil Augie is big enough to do his manly duties."

Then he thought of the lamp. No quarrel between lovers was authentic, in their circle, unless terminated by the man's hurling a lamp in the direction of the woman. So, accordingly, Augie reached for theirs and let it fly.

"You love me all that, Lil Augie?"

"Yea. All that an' mo' too."

"But you is leavin' me in de mawnin'."

"Yea, I gotta go. It's leavin'-time. But I'm gonna come back."

"You comin' back sho nuff?"

"Sho nuff, baby, I is."

But he knew it was not true. He knew he would rather die than set foot in St. Louis again. Furthermore, he did not love Della as he had at first thought. She wasn't proud enough. Even Augie could see that under the fine clothes she was cheap. He had liked her because she favored Florence, because he had vainly hoped that she would take Florence's place in his thoughts. But he now knew that Della was not Florence and never could be. And fine clothes would not do her any good.

X

IT WAS NEAR CHRISTMAS WHEN AUGIE
reached New Orleans again, and things were
sparkling for the Negroes. The eating-places and
hang-outs were crowded with country folks who
had come to town following the harvests. That
portion of the city blacks who worked in sugar
refineries or cotton fields during the warm
months in order to loaf throughout the winter
had returned. Everybody had money; everybody
was nigger-rich. A poker game was not respectable that had less than a hundred dollars in it.
Stevedores risked twenty-dollar gold pieces on a
single throw of the bones. Certain of the country
folks tossed all their nickels and pennies into the
gutter in order to keep their pockets from becoming cluttered.

But despite the general affluence, Augie could

buy and sell the other blacks by the dozen. His earnings had gone into the thousands. More important than that, his name had risen like a young star; he had become famous.

He and Bad-foot went directly to the barber shop. There they described the St. Louis fancy women to the home-staying fellows. They talked about the Cotton Flower Ball and boasted of Augie's success in taking the cake. Some of the drifters wanted to get tips on horses. Augie assumed an indifference to such questions, but he warned his followers to keep an eye on a young colt named Silver Heels, a recent addition to the Woodbine stables, and a great favorite of Augie's.

The talk switched to other things, and when, a bit later, Mississippi entered the shop, Augie promptly drew him into a corner and asked about Florence.

"I don't know much," Mississippi said. "I ain't got de job no mo'."

"How come dat, Mis'sippi?"

The old frock-tailed Negro seemed embarrassed. "Mistah Woody ain't got Florence now; he done quits."

"Oh! I on'erstand."

"Seems lak his people got wind about it; so he had to duck."

"Lissen, Mis'sippi. You reckon I could ease in *now?*"

"I don't know, Lil Augie. Anuther white man been makin' up to her, but he ain't as fine as Mistah Woody."

"Who he?"

"Gummy, de saloon man."

Augie's lip turned. "Where's yo' rig, Mis' sippi?"

"Down de street a lil piece."

"Come on. Us gonna drive over there."

Half an hour later Augie knocked boldly at Florence's door. Mississippi remained in the high seat. Autumn had touched the leaves of the trees. They kept falling on the old rig, falling like flakes of gold through the transparent golden light. In these fading surroundings, Augie seemed as brilliant as a spring flower. He was dressed in bottle-green with a canary vest and canary spats over pearl-buttoned shoes.

"I jes' come back," he told Florence.

"How you lak St. Louis?"

"There ain't nuthin' there for me. No peace."

"So you come back on account o' dat?"

"De season is done finish," he said. "I'm gonna be heah a long time, an' I wants yo' company, yella gal."

"How you know I don't b'long to somebody else, Lil Augie?"

"If it ain't Mistah Woody, it don't matter," he said.

Florence stood erect between the dark plush curtains of her front room. She was much taller than Little Augie. She was slim and proud-like, and her crimson painted mouth was beautiful against buff-colored skin. Augie's heart leapt as he watched her. His dream seemed so near he could almost put his hands on it.

"You ain't ask me do I love you, Lil Augie."

His diamonds shook nervously. "I ain't askin' a heap, yella gal."

"You is got enough money to ask for de moon. They tells me you got mo' spikes than Carter is got oats, Lil Augie."

"An' I'm fixin' to spend 'em all on you. I'm gonna make you lucky too."

"Is dat truf?"

"Sho, I was borned wid a veil. I'm lucky, an' everybody whut takes up wid me gets lucky."

"We might could be sweet," she said.

When Augie came out of the house a little later he was swollen like a pouter pigeon.

"This heah is gonna be ma house," he told Mississippi. "I done made maself a home. Come back in de mawnin' an' you can have yo' old job back again."

For the next few days Augie and Florence were always together. Florence, the insolent well-kept girl whom young Horace Church-Woodbine had been smitten on, was pointed out all over town with Little Augie, the sparkling nigger-rich jockey. There was something insulting in the match, something humiliating to the friends of the wealthy sportsman. But Augie was unconscious of it. All he knew was that Florence was the yellowest and best-looking gal he had ever seen and that he loved her worse than a horse loves corn.

In the evening she made him sweetened water and kept filling his glass while he pumped the accordion and sang. Florence did not sing. Augie thought that that was just as well; a girl as fine as

Florence needed no other talents. Besides, he felt able to supply enough music for both of them. So he sang for her the new tunes he had learned on Targee Street, sang them over and over again, and his heart was so big and swollen with pleasure he thought it would surely burst.

Wind was coming in from the Gulf with increasing strength, and all through the cool evening crisp gold leaves fell with a tiny clang and rattle against the windows and the door. Augie and Florence spent the hours examining new winter velvets that he had bought her. Recently, money had been short in her house; she had bought no new clothes in months. It gave Augie pleasure to supply these; he outdid himself for lavishness. Nothing was too expensive.

Finally, it was arranged for him to move into Florence's house—the house Mr. Woody had given her. Two full trunks were sent ahead. His remaining possessions he packed in a new wicker suitcase. This with the accordion he proposed to carry himself in the carriage. While Mississippi waited at the door, Augie took leave of Bad-foot.

"Us ain't gonna bus' up, Bad-foot. Us is always

gonna be lak dis." He held up his first two fingers.

"I gonna miss you jes' de same," Bad-foot said. "You is ma luck stone, son."

"You is good luck yo' black self," Augie smiled.

"I donno." Bad-foot rubbed his slick head with a hard stubby hand. "I donno 'bout me."

"I do. An' us gonna stay lak dis—no matter whut!"

Augie moved into Florence's house about midday. About midnight she moved out. The white neighbors, along with Gummy and other hostile persons, hastily formed a charge of immorality against the girl as soon as they understood. Florence had been too frankly a white man's girl. There was nothing to do but go.

So together she and Augie took a simple shack on the far fringes of the city, a shack behind a thicket on a yellow golden road near a railroad track. It was too far away from the heart of town for convenience, but there were trees on the roadside, and the air was full of birds. In the thickets there were turkeys the color of gun metal with red enameled heads, and in the road grouse dusting their wings nervously.

Mississippi had come with them. Each day he drove Augie in to the city. Often he returned again with both of them in the evening. Most of their time, it seemed, was spent in the carriage. And Florence did not enjoy it.

All of a sudden bad days came upon Little Augie. An accumulation of bad luck, reserved from many, many days past, fell at once upon his head. For years a successful gambler, he was now unable to draw a single pair from a deck of cards. All the dice that had been so responsive to his cajoling now seemed loaded against him.

In the races his horses stumbled, wrenched their legs, or otherwise failed. Mr. Woody turned spiteful and assigned him to all the impossible mounts. Even Bad-foot, now a trainer and a person of some authority in the stables, seemed distant.

Augie began drinking more than usual. He could not bear to confront his wretched fortunes with a clear mind. He could not bear to look Florence in the face. She had expected so much of him; he had promised so much.

In his misery he returned again and again to the stables; the horses reassured him. As long as he had their mute sympathy, the comfort of their presence, he would never lose hope. Somehow his love of Florence seemed fleeting and unessential, a mere frill on his life, when he was near the horses. As much as he desired to make a fine impression on her, he knew that he would be utterly cast down if he failed. He was no simpering pie-backed nigger who lived by women. He was a race-horse man. A woman was like a fine suit of clothes to him, something to please his vanity, to show him off well in the eyes of his friends.

"Damn 'em all, all de womens! I b'lieve Florence is bad luck to me anyhow."

But that was just mouth-talk. He had hardly spoken the words when he wondered if he were not actually losing his mind about her. How otherwise could he have imagined such an outlandish lie! He sought his accordion.

> Oh, de boat's gone up de river
> An' de tide's gone down.

XI

ALL THAT WINTER AUGIE FOUGHT OFF
bad luck. He carried a good-luck "hand" in his
coat pocket and a money "hand" in his pants—
small wads of cloth containing loadstones and
other magic ingredients mixed by a conjurer and
sewed up tight.

The next spring he went to Louisville for a
series of races to be climaxed by the Swanee
Handicap. Florence went with him, and a host of
stragglers and petty gamblers also followed.
Among them was Count Ragsdale.

With the decline of his fortunes, Augie had
gone into gambling with increasing hope. Thus,
striving to rehabilitate himself, he sank deeper
and deeper, his normal earnings, still unusual for
a black of those times, promptly melting in his
hand. He recalled a little hard-luck refrain.

Arna Bontemps

I don't gamble, I don't see
How ma money gets away from me.

But of course he did gamble. Bad luck had simply overtaken him.

However, when the time of the Swanee Handicap approached and the town became full of elegant people from all parts of the country, when every beggar on the street began giving his opinion of the relative horses and riders, Little Augie temporarily forgot his misfortunes. Here was a race more spectacular than any he had yet entered. It was a race that drew the best two-year-olds in seven states and was awaited with keen interest by thousands and thousands of people.

Once more his courage stood erect. He felt that he had been given a single flaming opportunity to recapture his past happiness.

Augie had lost a certain touch; a certain grace had slipped away. But if he could win this Handicap race, he told himself, nothing else would matter.

In the brilliant afternoon gay crowds of fine people filled the grandstand, wealthy society people from New Orleans, St. Louis, and Chicago. In

the center of the track there stood a gigantic
Maypole. Beneath it, on the inside lawns, women
sat with colored parasols. And on a small platform, in full view of all, a large floral horseshoe
stood, awaiting the winner.

Presently a uniformed trumpeter marched out
and blew a military signal. This was followed by a
stirring march rhythm from the band, during
which the parade of the horses to the barrier
began. A file of gorgeous animals left the pad-
dock. From Texas had come a promising entry
called Roan Knight. A beautiful filly, Revelation,
had a host of backers among the Kentucky
crowd. These two, with the flashy colt, Silver
Heels, to which Augie was assigned, were conceded the best chances of victory.

"This heah is fas' company," Augie told his
horse as they walked past the cheering crowds.
"You can't stop to nibble grass dis day. No, suh,
us gotta get up an' shout. I feels ma luck comin'
down. Us gotta shine dis day."

They marched slowly around the oval, the
high-strung horses threatening repeatedly to
break away, the jockeys restraining them with
obvious difficulty. Augie's horse wore blinkers

and a scarlet hood. In a moment the file had reached the barrier. From the platform with the floral horseshoe, the starter brought a flag downward with a sudden sweeping motion. In the same instant the sixteen finely trained animals reared and broke like one. The were off.

Meanwhile, in a Negro gambling-place, Count Ragsdale was receiving bets and placing them over the telephone. He was sitting in a small bare room, a room with a desk in one end, a few *Police Gazette* pictures on the walls, and a small writing-board tacked above the desk.

As the time for the race approached a little crowd of interested Negroes began to gather. Florence was among them. She stepped across to the desk and fished a roll of paper money from her stocking.

"Heah, Rags," she said. "Heah is some mo'. It ain't too late, is it?"

"No, not yet."

"Augie said, 'Let everything ride'; so heah it goes."

"He gonna be ridin' a good hoss."

"Ain't no hoss good enough to lay all you can scrape an' borrey on. But since things is lak they is, Augie say we jes' as well to die hard."

" 'Spose he lose, yellow gal?"

"Everything Lil Augie got is ridin' wid him. Tha's de way he done fix it. If he lose, he lose."

"Hm. Everything goes. But I'm sho pullin' ma left teat that he won't lose."

The betting was finished, and the little crowd became excited, waiting for the first reports to come in over the telephone. Florence sat on the edge of the desk in a voluminous yellow silk dress. She was wearing a red hat and red shoes. Rags ogled her as he held the receiver to his ear.

Suddenly Rags shouted, "He say they's at de barrier!"

Then a moment's hush. From every angle, round eyes were fixed on him, a terrible inquisition of round white eyes. Florence seemed unmoved, but her toe twitched. The eyes grew in number, increased in size, and drew nearer.

"He say they is off."

There was a silence the duration of a long breath.

Then: "They breaks well. They's in a pack. He

say Revelation gets loose; she's a fast sprinter, he say, she is settin' de pace. Behin' her comes Roan Knight. Silver Heels gets loose; he says Lil Augie is movin' into a position to challenge de leaders. At de quarter: Revelation, Roan Knight, an' Silver Heels, in that order."

There was another silence.

"He say Roan Knight an' Silver Heels is neck an' neck. They is three lengths ahead of de nearest rival; they's one length behin' Revelation. As they approach de half, he say, de young filly is losin' her lead. De other two is at her heels. They all three is neck to neck. Silver Heels leads Roan Knight by a head as they flash into de stretch. Revelation has fallen back.

"He say they's on de stretch, Lil Augie whippin' hard, fightin' to hold his lead. They's neck to neck.

"Roan Knight wins by a wink!"

Florence waited for Augie in their room, her hat on, her trunk packed. The room looked empty. She had left Augie nothing but a few clothes and his instrument. Everything that could be transformed into money was in her trunk: jewelry, trinkets, Augie's gold-hilted canes, and the best of his suits.

Augie staggered into the room as modestly as a stranger. He paid no attention to what he saw. Florence got up and commenced walking to and fro, a summer parasol in her hand.

"I'm gonna quit you, Lil Augie," she said.

"How come dat, yella gal?"

"Yo' luck done change, Lil Augie. It's leavin'-time."

Suddenly he looked tired and old. "Yea, ma luck done gone down."

"It's leavin'-time."

"Hm. Putty yella womens lak you ain't made for onlucky niggers."

"It's more'n a notion, Lil Augie. I done got used to havin' things. Y'all men done spoilt me."

"It's leavin'-time, yella gal, but where is you goin'?"

"To St. Louis. Rags is gonna take me."

"Oh."

"He is havin' luck."

"Well, if you mus', you mus'. But 'member dis: I wouldn't let dat gold-toothed nigger take you 'way so slick if ma luck was in. I'd fight 'bout you; I'd fight ma daddy 'bout you. But ma luck is done gone down."

After Florence drove away, Augie put what remained of his fine clothes into the wicker suit-case and wrapped his accordion in newspaper. The summer twilight was just falling. He wore the Prince Albert and top-hat; it was the only outfit Florence had left him.

Then suddenly he gathered his luggage and left the house, walking toward the railroad track. A tiny disconsolate man, he climbed the embank-ment and set out between the rails. On and on he walked. Just ahead of him the horizon had a soft rose and gold flush. Dim pine woods stood motionless along the tracks, but he turned neither to one side nor to the other. His attention was fixed, like the attention of a man who has been witched.

In the distance, he suggested an insect crawl-ing toward the ultimate needle-point where the rails converge. Curiously, as his figure dimin-ished, the ironic silk hat seemed to wax larger and larger. In the end, it swallowed both man and luggage.

— PART TWO —

I

AN INCREDIBLE ORANGE MOON WAS RIS-
ing over a world that seemed tiny by comparison,
a world of low fences, dark shrubbery, and little,
crooked shacks.

Augie, standing against a whitewashed picket
gate, beneath the street lamp, suggested a comic
little man cut with scissors from black paper. His
preposterous luggage, his battered top-hat, were
both far out of proportion with his small, aged
body. He had rested a moment to re-fill his pipe
and to cast a few nervous glances over the
strange dark neighborhood.

"Dis de place a'right," he told himself. "But
how's I'm gonna find Leah at dis time o' night? I
ain't seen a livin' soul whut could enlighten me."

There was not a lighted window in sight, no
sound indicating that any one was awake any-

where around. Once again Augie cursed his wretched luck. Here he was, no telling how near Leah's home, with no way of finding her before morning. He would have preferred riding on in the box car from which he had dropped a few hours earlier to this miserable waiting and aimless wandering.

From the Los Angeles freight yards Augie had tramped down to Watts and thence found his way out to Mudtown, the Negro neighborhood on the edge of that suburb. He had come a great many miles to seek Leah, and he had actually been on his way a dozen years. Curiously, Fate had prolonged the intervals between the steps of his journey, and he had lingered on and on in the intervening cities—San Antonio, Austin, Waco, Santa Fe, Albuquerque, Tucson, and Phoenix. Sometimes the end had seemed far away, so far indeed that the hope of ever reaching it became dim. Yet each time it would finally rise up again like a young flame, and Augie would become restless and dissatisfied with his surroundings. Invariably, at such times, he caught the first west-bound freight train.

And at last he was in Mudtown. This section

before the blacks came, had evidently been a walnut grove. A few of the trees were still standing. Beneath them crude shacks had been built and vines—morning-glory, gourd, and honeysuckle—had promptly covered them, giving the whole neighborhood an aspect of savage wildness. Elsewhere shacks were built in clumps of castor-bean trees and thus almost completely hidden away.

The streets of Mudtown were three or four dusty wagon paths. In the moist grass along the edges cows were staked. Broken carts and useless wagons littered the front yards of the people, carts with turkeys and game chickens and guinea fowl roosting on the spokes of the wheels and wagons from the beds of which small dark mules were eating straw. Ducks were sleeping in the weeds, and there was on the air a suggestion of pigs and slime holes. Tiny hoot-owls were sitting bravely on fence posts while bats wavered overhead like shadows.

Augie got in the middle of the road and started back toward the railroad tracks again. A small dog crept from under a step and came yapping out at him. There were gnats in the air. Augie staggered on the rough road like a drunken man, stumbling in numerous chuck-holes and bruising his shins. But he plodded steadily ahead.

In those days, fifteen or twenty years ago, Negroes were not plentiful in the far west. Least of all were they to be seen in the rural parts. A few of them, to be sure, had come as early as the historical gold rush with the forty-niners, working in personal service. Others had followed the conquest of the frontier. But the number had remained small until the great transcontinental railway lines established important terminals in Los Angeles and San Francisco. Then the real migration began. First the railroad men, Pullman porters and dining-car waiters, brought their families; hearing the rumors of attractive working conditions, their friends followed. Still the tendency was for them to remain in the larger centers and particularly in the locality of the train yards.

The small group in Mudtown was exceptional. Here, removed from the influences of white folks, they did not acquire the inhibitions of their city brothers. Mudtown was like a tiny section of the deep south literally transplanted. Throughout the warm summer days old toothless men sat in front of the little grocery store on boxes, chewing the stems of cob pipes, recalling the 'Mancipation, the actual beginning of their race. Women cooked over fireplaces in the yards and boiled their clothes in heavy iron kettles. There were songs in the little frail houses and over the steaming pots. Lilacs grew at every doorstep. In every house there was a guitar.

Augie, of course, was not interested in these features of the place. He was seeking his sister Leah, returning home. Under a shed at an unimportant railroad flag station, he found a crowd of tramps sleeping on the ground. He looked at them a moment scornfully, then went around to the back and rested his luggage. He remembered the large bottle under his coat and took a long drink. He was not sleepy.

"Come on up, Mistah Sun," he said. "Heah I is at de gates o' home. Heah I is, waitin' for day to break. Like as not I done been pas' Leah's door two o' t'ree times an' didn't know it. I'm gettin' fidgety now. Come on up, Mistah Sun!"

Arna Bontemps

Suddenly over the pulsing countryside the trumpeting of innumerable cocks tore the air. Somewhere a train whistled. Some morning birds burst unexpectedly into singing. Augie felt a quick excitement. His heart pounded against his ribs.

"It's comin' up," he exclaimed. "Day gonna break 'fo' you can say 'Jack Robinson.' O Mistah Sun!"

II

LEAH'S HOUSE, ACROSS THE SWAMP FROM Mudtown, faced the railroad track. It was the same little whitewashed house to which she had come when she left St. Louis in the days when her children were youngsters and Augie was a figure on Targee Street. The house was built on a narrow strip of black land that fronted Bingham Road and sloped gradually back to the swamp. There was a small barn, a few fruit trees, and some eucalyptuses of Leah's own planting which now touched the sky.

Leah's houseful of children was long gone. She was alone except for Terry, the son of her dead daughter Ida. This timid fifteen-year-old boy did the yard chores and otherwise looked after the place, which, but for him, would have been destroyed by weeds. For Pig, Leah's youngest son and the last to leave her, had recently got himself a wife, moved into the heart of Mudtown, and promptly lost the sense of responsibility he had formerly had for his mother's place.

On the morning following Augie's first night in Mudtown the old black woman and the boy were sitting at a little kitchen table, eating hot biscuits with bacon grease and molasses. The sun was coming up strong, and there was the promise of a hot day.

Suddenly, while they faced each other quietly across the red-checkered table cover, Little Augie appeared in the door frame—a tiny withered man in a frayed and ancient Prince Albert and a badly battered silk hat, carrying in one hand a dilapidated wicker traveling-bag and in the other the familiar accordion.

Leah got up and stood in the middle of the floor as if paralyzed. Augie felt her looking through him as through a ghost or a puff of smoke. For all he knew, she might have been counting the heifers in the barnyard or watching the pigs tunnel beneath the straw pile. But more than likely she was trying to see him as he used to be, as she remembered him. Then suddenly water filled her eyes, and he knew by that that she was convinced of what she saw.

"Dis me, Leah," he said in a thin, exhausted voice. "Lil Augie."

Leah hugged him and carried on as if she were his real mother and he still a child.

"Lawd, boy, it sho is you. Done dropped out o' de sky, right in front o' our door."

Augie couldn't speak.

"Dis Ida's boy," Leah told him, indicating Terry. "Ain't he fine?"

" 'Deed so." Augie's eyes had become defective; he seemed to be looking over the tops of imaginary spectacles.

"An' ask me is he smart. Hm! Smart as a whup."

"Looka heah! Head taller den me." Augie was speaking to Terry. "How old is you?"

"Fifteen," Terry said.

"Do tell. Time sho flies."

Augie was given a shed room which had been unused since the last of Leah's children left home. It was attached like an afterthought to the house and was entered from the outside. It had no actual connection with any of the other rooms, and its furnishings consisted of a small bed and washstand with an old-fashioned bowl and pitcher. There would have been room for very little more. The single window was above Augie's reach and fastened so that it could not be opened.

Unpacking his luggage here, Augie carefully brought out the bottle of whiskey and placed it on the commode. Then he unwrapped his accordion. These represented the complete remains of his character. Augie was fairly well worn out.

The next day Leah provided him with an outfit of old clothes left by her grown sons. In them Augie was, of course, lost. He raised the pants by shortening a pair of home-made galluses; the shoes looked formidable, but he wore them without apparent inconvenience.

"Where'd you get all dat car-fare?" Leah asked him at breakfast. They had been discussing his trip, and Augie had failed to clear this point.

Augie was in a fine spirit after a night of rest, but Leah's question made him squirm. Finally, however, he confessed with great shame that he had made the trip by freight train and that he had forgotten how many years had passed since he first turned his face westward.

Augie had not lived in the country since he was a boy on the Red River plantation, but he made himself immediately at home on Leah's place. He was not lazy or indolent in the easy nigger manner; Augie had to always be doing something, and he enjoyed the absurd picture he made doing the awkward yard chores. Coming up from the barn in the afternoon, he chuckled merrily: "Bet y'all didn't see me on dat ole haystack dis mawnin'."

"Who didn't?" Leah rolled her eyes.

Augie slapped his hip. "Doggone! I'm a fawmin' somebody from way back."

"Dat you is," Leah smiled. "Jes' mind out you don't stick yo'self, foolin' wid dat long pitch-fawk."

But Augie wouldn't be stopped. Just before dark he volunteered to milk Leah's old cow. Leah and Terry stood by, watching the fun. Carefully adjusting his stool, Augie put his hands on the cow's teats so lightly that he gave her the all-overs. When she began dancing he stroked her flanks reassuringly.

"Don't mind me, Boss," he said. "Saw. Saw now! 'Member, gal, I's yo' pappy."

Boss didn't remember. So Leah decided that Augie had better not bother with the milking. Fooling around like that with a cow's teats was a bad thing to do. It would sometimes cause the animal to withhold her milk altogether. Augie, if he persisted, would have Boss so that even Leah could not milk her.

That evening after dark Augie finished his bottle of whiskey. Then, when the other folks had gone to bed, he slipped out beneath the charcoal shadows with his accordion. Sitting beside a tree, he began improvising softly on the instrument, touching occasionally fragments of familiar melodies and coloring them gayly with his own bright emotions.

A stir of ocean air followed the warm day. Later the moon whitened the orchard, disclosing the little man in his incongruous oversized clothes, showered by blossoms.

"I is lucky again," he told himself. "Dis is de Lil Augie whut *usta* be. Ma luck is comin' down, an' it sho feels good."

Augie was still inordinately fond of horses. He doted on them with the enthusiasm of other old men for the chippies on the water front. They reminded him of his youth, his childish arrogance, and the admiring cronies who had fled from him.

Late one afternoon a sudden June wind shook from the trees a quantity of green fruit. When the orchard was still again Augie nervously filled his pipe and took a basket to gather apples from the ground. Seeing him among the trees, Leah shouted from her window: "Don't bring nara one o' dem in heah. They ain't fitten to eat lak they is, an' I sho ain't fixin' to make no p'serves yet—not out o' dem sour things nohow."

"Ah, hush up, gal," Augie grumbled. "I ain't even studyin' 'bout you. These here apples is for Miss Ludy. They ain't all dat sour neither; I'm pickin' out de ripes' ones."

After a short while he started toward the barn with the half-filled basket. The sun had set. The twilight seemed like a blue mist about the fence and outhouses. Some guinea fowl were still awake in the bushes, but the chickens had found roosts. Several black pullets sat on the cross pieces of the big gate like notes on a music staff.

Augie came up beside the fence and called Miss Ludy, making a clucking sound with his tongue. The drowsy mare left her hay and came to him. Standing with one foot on a rail, Augie fed her the young fruit from his hand. Patient and apparently unconcerned, he stood there a long time, stroking the bony old face. Miss Ludy took the apples in her huge teeth and crushed them wearily.

Inside Leah told the youngster something about Augie's former life. An illiterate old woman, she knew nothing of the why's and wherefore's. She could not tell him that Augie's attachment to animals had begun during his childhood when, because of his inferior size and strength, he had been unable to hold his own with the rough black boys of his own age; that, removed from their company because of this, he learned to ride horses and finally acquired with them the influence he was unable to acquire with people. Blind to these causes, the wrinkled old woman nevertheless had her own thoughts.

"Sumpin' or other mus' be on Augie's mind,"

she said simply. "He always talk his troubles to de hosses—ever since he was a boy."

Then she told Terry what she knew of the old man's former life. Leah had lost track of him herself after his break-up with Florence. Augie's life, between that dim day and the day on which he appeared in Leah's doorway, battered and red-eyed, had been meaningless. During the interim he had become old. Yet, seemingly, nothing had happened. Somehow he had managed to keep one relic of his corrupted finery: the Prince Albert outfit.

The kitchen became quite dark. Leah finished talking and lit a lamp. The boy, still rapt, elbows on the table, sat silently facing her. The old woman had told the story intimately, whispering it like a secret. Augie was her "baby" brother.

Terry went outside; a big round moon confronted him from a low hill. In his mind, Augie took on a singular glamour. For the first time he felt his kinship with his great-uncle; he too loved horses, their warm unembarrassing presence. He saw the tiny man fancifully in the flame-bright shirts and shining boots he must have worn as a jockey. And while he thought, his own heartbeats marked the footfalls of dim racing horses.

Seeing Augie, the wreck he had become, the story seemed fantastic. Only the merest shadow of his former self remained. Terry came upon him at the fence—the empty basket upturned on the ground—still stroking the animal's shaggy mane. A glint of moonlight shone like phosphorus on his face and shoulders. The tiny old man looked into the horse's face sadly, like one remembering love. And it seemed as if water would drop out of his eyes.

III

"I DONE COME HOME AN' SETTLE DOWN
for life," Augie said.

He was standing beside the railroad embankment, pants drawn up under his arms and hat slipping over his ears, minding Leah's two young heifers. Once more he felt at peace with the whole world. The heifers were grazing in the wild alfalfa along the roadside. Meadow larks were singing on a dozen fence posts.

Augie climbed the embankment and considered the grass on the opposite slope. It was even greener than that on Leah's side. So he quickly gathered up his chains and led his charges over the rise and into the fresh pasture. He did not realize it then, but he was on enemy ground.

A huge black woman with a flat, ugly face was plowing with a team of mules in a field near the barbed-wire fence of the railroad. Her dress was tucked up above the knees, and she wore a red headcloth and a pair of heavy man's shoes. Her team seemed unusually disagreeable, and that made it necessary for her to keep shouting and popping the blacksnake whip.

Augie turned his back on her with disgust, sank his hands in his high pockets, and stood looking off in the opposite direction while the heifers grazed. Meanwhile the unfamiliar black woman circled the field and brought her team puffing along the fence near Augie. She stopped, came across the new furrows, and rested her foot on a strand of the fence wire. A moment she stood there quietly, her cheeks swollen with tobacco, chewing meditatively.

"Looka heah, ole man! Ain't they no grass on yo' side o' de road?"

Augie adjusted his pipe and spat. "Sho'. Plenty."

"Well, how come you don't keep yo' calfs over there?"

"It's mo' green on dis side. Tha's how come."

"It is, hunh? Well, you gonna keep 'em over there jes' de same. Us got a cow whut laks green grass too." She leaned across the fence and cut one of the heifers with her whip. "Git on, you young uns. Git on 'cross on yo' own side."

The heifers broke into a run, climbed the embankment, and started down the road. Augie, tugging at their chains, was hard pressed to keep them from running away. So he didn't get a chance to answer the woman. He was fighting mad. But when he got the heifers quieted she had returned to her plow and was going down the field.

"Damn dat black cat," he said. "I feels just lak gettin' me a ax handle an' beatin' her brains out."

The folks whose place the woman Tisha was plowing lived in a whitewashed shack behind a clump of red castor-bean trees. The family, peasants migrated from Texas, consisted now of Clara Clow, the mother, and her two daughters, Beulah and Azilee. They alone remained of a larger family that had come to Bingham Road in a wagon nearly ten years earlier. Tisha had also been in that wagon as one of the family, but now she was a grown woman and lived across a little spiky pasture in a hut of her own near a muddy watering-place.

Recently Tisha's life had been considerably altered. One day while she was working the mules beneath the low fruit trees a smut-colored derelict named Lissus had come down the railroad tracks and stopped to chew the rag with her beside the fence. He was almost naked, having on but two pieces of clothing—a greasy red undershirt and a pair of ragged pants. And the tips of his shoes had been cut away in order to free his long toes. He was hungry and fairly worn out from tramping.

Lissus told Tisha that he had come from Arizona, where he had been working in the mines near a border town. He was in hard luck and wanted something to eat. She sent him to the barn to wait. Later, when she had unhitched the mules, she brought him some stale biscuits and a pot of coffee. Both tasted mighty good to a hungry man, so good indeed that Lissus licked his lips when the pot was empty.

"M-m. Dat sho' touched de spot," he said.

"It wa'n't nuthin'," Tisha said. "Anything is good when you's hongry."

"Wha, wha! Don't put dat out," he laughed. "I knows good biscuits when I tastes 'em. I bet you stuck yo' ole sweet finger in de coffee an' dat was how come *it* was so good."

"Ah, go on, ole greedy man! You's jes' hongry."

Lissus found a stopping-place in Mudtown. And day after day he returned to pass words with Tisha by the fence, under the low trees or in the corn rows. In the early evening they sat on a pile of fodder behind the cow pen, laughing and amusing themselves. He was such a wretched sight in his rags that Tisha would not allow him to enter the Clows' house; so at first she slept with him in the barn. Later they took the small deserted hut and lived together beyond the pasture, across the sandy back fields from the Clows' house.

Lissus, however, was a fellow who liked to fly about, and Tisha did not immediately succeed in clipping his wings. He was at home one week and gone the next. There were other irregularities also in his conduct, but all in all the two were as contented as swine. Near their hut there was a thicket of tall weeds and the leaky watering-trough. Here the old bony steers of the pasture rested and hid from the sun. And here mosquitoes came and multiplied.

Soon Tisha and Lissus made some friends on the edge of Mudtown. Among them were two or three young women who lived in a small abandoned store building beneath a single black pine tree near the edge of the swamp and carried on a suspicious business. All that the neighbors knew about these black girls was that they went about the place during the day in dirty kimonos with their hair wild and uncombed like the hair of savages and that they had a phonograph that played low-down blues at all hours of the night. They were hideous crowlike females, precisely of Tisha's stamp, and with them she and Lissus were completely happy. In the evenings the two frequently walked to Mudtown, circling the swamp, and spent half the night in the little building. Invariably, during these visits, they got drunk and came home down the middle of the dusty road shouting and screaming wildly, staggering and kicking up their heels in the moonlight. It was all the recreation they required outside their own hut.

But it came to an end. At length one of the women set her mind on Lissus and contrived to get him away from Tisha. Tisha's little shoe-button eyes were wide open. She caught the chippie trying to clip a piece of Lissus' shirt tail. That was conclusive evidence of her design. Tisha knew that a piece of a man's shirt, sewed into a charm, was about the best thing in the world to win his love, and she thought it was terribly deceitful of her friend to attempt it on Lissus. It grieved her so badly, in fact, that she immediately lost her mind, and the first thing she knew she had the girl by the hair, shaking her as if she were a Topsy doll. The quarrel quickly spread, the other girls taking a hand in it, and as a result Tisha had to knock the teeth out of one black head and threaten to knife another. So by the time Augie met her, Tisha and Lissus were at peace with the world. They had no friends and they had no problems.

A few moments after his words with Tisha, Augie gathered up his chains again and led the heifers farther down the road where he could not even see the ugly black woman and her mules. But Augie's mind had been upset by Tisha, and he could not feel easy again, no matter how far he went. He knew he had an enemy across the railroad track, and the thought troubled him. Suddenly all the birds left the fence posts. The heifers became restless and hard to manage. There was no need to keep them out longer. Augie led them into the center of the road and started home.

"Le's get on in now," he said to the glossy young animals. "Us been out too long. Y'all gals is gettin' beside yo'self."

A few days later Augie met Tisha again. Leah had sent him out with a scythe to reap a bit of the summer hay that grew so abundantly on the railroad land along the tracks. It was fast becoming too tall for grazing; the heifers only trampled and spoiled it. So Augie was out before breakfast, a whetstone in his pocket, preparing to lay swale. Crossing the tracks near the Clows' fence, he again caught sight of the black woman. She was coming down a corn row with a singletree in her hand.

Seeing her, Augie promptly put the scythe back on his shoulder and turned to go home.

Tisha called, "Hey there, ole man!"

Augie paused to listen but did not speak.

"How come you turns round an' go home when you see me?"

"It's too soon in de mawnin'," he said. "Too soon in de mawnin' to look at a woman whut's black an' ugly as you is. It's onlucky."

Tisha foamed at the mouth.

"Where you get on at, callin' somebody black. You lil ole piece o' man, you."

Augie started away again.

"Devil take ma unhardlucky soul," he mumbled. "Heah I got to go an' see dat bad-luck cat de first thing in de mawnin'. I jes' as well's to go home. There ain't no use tryin' to work wid dat kind o' luck followin' you."

No amount of entreaty on the part of Leah would induce him to leave the yard again that day. Something might happen to him, he told her. He knew bad luck when he saw it, and he didn't intend to take any unnecessary chances. In his place Leah had to send the boy Terry to do the reaping. The youngster was glad to go; so Augie went to his room and took a long nap to kill time.

In the afternoon, when he awakened, as he stood in the doorway stretching his old rattling bones, Augie saw the boy returning on the railroad tracks with the two young Clow girls, Beulah and Azilee. It was Augie's first glimpse of these neighbors, though they were frequently mentioned in the conversation of Leah and Terry. They were big healthy-looking brown girls about sixteen and seventeen, very countrified in their appearance, with barbarous unstraightened hair. But they wore clean, stiff-pressed ginghams and seemed to Augie rather fine against that rustic background.

"Looka heah, hush!" he exclaimed. "Them gals is first rate. Business gonna pick up now."

He walked up the path and waited at the gate for the young people. They came down the embankment, laughing at the top of their voices. A smile split Little Augie's face from ear to ear. His sparse yellow teeth were shamelessly exposed. He jerked his old hat off with sudden exaggerated swagger and all but broke his back bowing.

IV

AFTER THAT FIRST BRIEF MEETING AT THE gate, Augie saw nothing of the Clow girls for several days. Things were quiet on Bingham Road. Brooding. The fever and toil of giving birth was everywhere manifest. The dark earth became warm and throbbed. Young leaves colored the trees of the orchard. In the hedges a spirited twittering persisted. Disagreeable hens, sitting on large nests of eggs, complained bitterly.

Every day Augie examined a plot where he and Terry and Leah had planted a new garden. They had worked almost a week, preparing the soil and dropping the seeds. And now that it was done, Augie began to feel a touching interest in the results. Finally, along a fence where Kentucky Wonders were planted, he saw a row of tiny white shoulders rounded above the surface. With determined faith they labored all morning; then, toward noon, the stronger ones succeeded in bringing small heads through the crusted loam. The next day Augie found that the young plants had extended pairs of new leaves like little bird wings and seemed about to fly.

There were curious doings around the barn; the heifers were cutting up. Understanding this behavior, Augie arranged for their "service," and the following evening he and Terry led two of them away. They came, after a long dusty walk, to a gate with the sign: *Bull, Holstein.* The animal stood in a small muddy pen and was so terrible that he could not be approached. The owner handled him by means of a pole attached to a ring in the nose. Restraining him thus over the wooden walls of the pen, the gate was opened and the clean sleek heifers led in singly. They seemed too young and glossy, but they were apparently unafraid.

Augie and the owner, sitting on the fence, laughed together, matching ribaldries. To Terry, his great-uncle seemed ridiculous, trying to carry on in this hearty manner. He was so gentle and soft-spoken that obscene language seemed unnatural coming from him. But his fluency indicated that he was not unaccustomed to it.

Returning home, Augie said, "De next thing us got on dock is to find de right kind o' stallion for Miss Ludy."

"Whut kind you mean?" Terry asked.

"Hm. Tha's de point. I ain't sayin' a word to Leah, but I got plans. Plans whut won't do to tell."

He became meditative. It was almost dark in the road. As they walked the dust kicked up by the heifers stood at their backs like a cloud. When the boy understood that Augie did not intend to divulge more he said: "You can tell me. I won't say nuthin' about it."

"I'm jes' studyin'," Augie said. "You might could help me some too." He grew more confidential. "You see it's lak dis: Miss Ludy usta be a race hoss; I seen it from de mark. She all wore out now. But de colt!"

"I see," Terry said.

Augie chuckled and hunched the boy with his sharp little elbow.

"You on'erstand everything. One dese days us gonna be on Easy Street. All we needs is a fancy stallion for dat ole lady of ours."

Terry of course did not doubt that Augie was right about Miss Ludy's blood or the possibility of breeding her with another fancy horse. But it was to be a secret. So when they reached home they said nothing more about it.

Augie had intended to make investigations the following day, but something else turned up, and the plans for Miss Ludy were neglected. Leah broke her spectacles. She had only infrequent use for them, but this afternoon she was about to begin some needlework. If she sewed at night by the kerosene lamp, they would be necessary. Of late she had not been sewing much, and it had been years since she last made a patch quilt. But now that she had Augie and Terry to help her and plenty of time, there was no reason why she should not improve the hours.

After dinner she sent Augie to Watts to have new eyes put in the old frame. The distance was not more than two miles, and Augie chose to walk. Wearing the little Prince Albert again, he set out on the road with far more assurance than he had exhibited when he first came up that road to Leah's house a few weeks earlier. He walked with an important air, his head raised and his arms swinging.

The authority he had so quickly gained in the barnyard was already having its effect. It was bringing to light a shadow of the little arrogant man who died in him thirty years before. The presence of Miss Ludy and the promise of a handsome colt was all that he needed. He set his bruised and ancient hat cockily on the side of his head and disappeared beyond a rise in the road.

"Augie ain't de same pusson," Leah remarked, seeing him vanish. "He done blossom out since he come home."

When Augie returned from Watts, shortly before dark, he was covering the entire road. Reeling from one side to the other, arms flying and the tails of his coat in the wind, he cut a lugubrious figure. At the gate finally he paused, resting on its support, and calmly examined in retrospect the perilous journey he had made. He was not merely fatigued; flames in his eyes indicated a very bad temper as well.

Questioned by Leah in the kitchen, he was unable to tell anything whatever about the spectacles. She, however, searched his pockets and found them inside the coat. She also discovered a formidable bottle of whiskey. Augie did not remember that he had either and so did not protest when Leah took the bottle along with the spectacles.

Augie, despite his drunkenness and temper, was still deferential to his sister. His strength exhausted, he surrendered himself into a chair and dropped his head forward on his chest, his hands dangling between his knees.

The sight disgusted Leah.

"Ain't you shame o' yo'self, now!" she said, arms akimbo on her hips.

"I don't feel good," he pleaded. "Don't p-pester me."

"You is low, jes' a low nigger. You ain't no man. You ain't nuthin'."

At first he did not appear to be listening. Then he raised his head, answering feebly: "S-'sa lie. Where you get dat 'low' stuff? I behaves maself; I

stays at home; I works hard an' saves ma money;
I wears good clo's. I ain't crazy. I got s-sense."

Leah lost her patience. "You betta hush dat
drunk mouf 'fo' Jesus strike you blind," she said.

"Hm. Jesus love me de same way he do you,"
Augie argued. "Damn if he don't."

V

WHILE IN WATTS ON HIS ERRAND FOR LEAH,
Augie got a bit of news from Mudtown that made
a sharp impression on his mind. It seemed that
big doings were cooking in that neighborhood.
The railroad men, Pullman car porters and dining-
car waiters, were about to give their annual picnic
and dance. It was an event in those days, an event
so popular with the local blacks that their reports
of it filled the old fellow with an excitement
keener than he had felt in years. So he immediately determined to go. But he decided to keep his
plans to himself and perhaps surprise the young
folks by his presence. He had felt, of late, that
Terry and the Clow girls considered him an old
has-been. It would do him good to give them a
surprise. So while the youngsters were making

plans to attend he stood apart and kept his thoughts to himself.

Green Lake, the dance-hall park on the edge of Mudtown, had formerly been the house and yard of the farmer in whose walnut grove the small neighborhood had sprung up. Now, with flying-horses and a small wooden dance pavilion, it was the most satisfactory place in the vicinity for the colored outings and dances. Aside from the times when it was secured for such frolics, it was opened but once a week. On these days Negro and Mexican children flocked there in Sunday school clothes, enchanted by the painted horses, the flags, and the little mechanical organ. That one horse lacked a tail and one a foreleg and that others were losing their manes meant nothing to their ardor. They pressed one another noisily in the line, their tiny fingers perspiring and sticky from grasping pennies.

There was little here to amuse grown-ups. But for the occasion of the railroad men's picnic special preparations were made. A small carnival company set up a row of gaming concessions in canvas tents. The gypsies who usually camped on the fringes of the grove drew near and opened a booth beneath the trees. And, not to be outdone, Negroes came with things to sell: pig's feet, craw-daddies, baked sweet potatoes, corn on the cob, slices of watermelon, lemonade. The odors from their steaming kettles filled the air.

It was afternoon when the big crowd began to arrive. In the clear sunlight their gay clothes made a striking pageant against the green yards of Mudtown. That morning a fog swept the tree-tops and roof gables, but it passed quickly as the day warmed and the women came with sun para-sols and fans. A few of the country folks arrived in wagons and buggies, but the larger part of the crowd walked. Though wearing new shoes, many of which had high heels and were painful, the young women were loud and cheerful.

Terry went with the Clow girls in the late after-noon. But he had been in Mudtown in his Uncle Pig's house all morning and had watched the early ones with great amusement as they passed. In the first rush a young mulattress with enor-mous hips minced along painfully. A beribboned hat dangled on her arm and ribbons streamed from her shoulders and from her waist. A puny-looking boy, half her size and dull black, escorted her slowly and with commendable patience. At every few paces she paused to rest. She was not one to make a secret of her misery; her feet were bothering her, and as she approached Pig's gate Terry saw that she had perspired freely, the moisture staining her silk dress beneath the arms and on the shoulders.

"I do so hate hot weather," she was telling her companion. "I nachally can't stan' it. It's on 'count o' me bein' so plump-lak, I reckon."

He smiled, showing a little embarrassment.

"Tha's a' right, baby. Jes' take it easy; us got plenty o' time. You know them raw-bony gals ain't no good in de wintertime. Tha's when you shines."

"Too, I has a lil trouble wid ma feet. Standin' so much, you know. Some days I be's on ma feet from mawnin' to night. It's mighty hard on we heavy-set gals."

"Hm. I on'erstand everything. I'm a Pullman porter maself, an' them movin' trains is sumpin' or other on de dogs too."

Terry thought of the anecdotes he had so often heard the railroading fellows tell among themselves about their feet after a hard run, about having to step off curbstones backwards to avoid pain, or crawling the last few steps home from the depot.

All day the brilliant colors of gaudy clothes flashed in the sun; reds predominated, violent sun-bright shades and the diminishing tones of strawberry, coral, and pink. The same old nigger taste, the same childlike love of color, was everywhere manifest.

Terry met the Clow girls just before sunset. Elbowing their way through the crowds, they began making a round of the booths. White men with hollow faces, tobacco-stained mouths, and hard rasping voices announced their games. Beside them stood stringy, middle-aged women, their faces grotesquely rouged, offering hoops and balls to the Negroes.

Through the lace trees, above the booths, the sunset showed softly. One by one the firm, straight light shafts withdrew, leaving the park in shadow. The odors of the steaming food stimulated appetites. Terry and the girls bought pig's feet and sat on a bench, away from the biggest crowd, to eat.

As the park darkened, a portion of the folks dispersed. The ironic flying horses of the merry-go-round stopped, their heads still unbended, and the exhausted young riders toppled from their backs. It became quite dark; beneath a remote tree where there had been a fire some coals glowed softly, uttering a faint smoke like breath.

Soon afterward the pavilion was lighted and the dance music commenced. When Terry and the girls followed the crowd inside a few couples were already on the floor. They were just warming to the vivid, slow-drag rhythm. The contagion seemed to spread in ripples. Here a toe tapped the floor, a little farther on a finger snapped; one by one the boys reached for their girls.

"How 'bout it, honey?"

"Suits me."

"Let's strut."

The couple standing next to Terry got off. The music halted for an instant on a high note as if uncertain—then decided. Clash! The cymbals came sharply together. Beulah took the movement. His arm around her waist, Terry's body made a corresponding curve.

A trombone, its gold throat pointed upward, rose above the other instruments, enlarged its mouth and cried. Suddenly the rough-board walls lost their security and the floor, dipping and tossing, seemed to float. Unaccustomed to frenzies of this sort, Terry was soon completely intoxicated. In the orchestra he saw the mouth of that horn like a barrel-head. Hidden behind it, the musician became a dwarf. A clarinet stretched the length of a man, and at the piano, the keyboard of which had assumed a crazy angle, two huge disembodied hands worked magic.

Beulah danced with easy grace; she knew the steps, but she was not self-conscious. As they circled the group, Beulah humming the melodies, Terry imagined that he could feel her body vibrate. He imagined that under the influence of music some compulsion other than her own will possessed her and directed her movements. He had often heard of such dancing.

During another dance Terry stood off to the side, steadying himself against a post. In the circle of dancers revolving before him he saw many who were perspiring, their straightened hair beginning already to crimp near the scalp where the moisture touched it. Again the pitiful, half-suppressed pain of tight shoes was everywhere evident.

A lean yellow boy, wearing a candy-striped shirt and a box coat, came over to Terry. When he smiled he exhibited a row of gold teeth. Terry knew that the fellow was easing around in order to dance with Beulah and Azilee. He walked with a slight affectation, appearing to favor one foot. But not in the manner of a lame person.

"Whut's de matter?" Terry asked pleasantly. "Feet hurt?"

"Nah," the boy grinned. "Feet don't hurt; jes' got a lil seam in ma sock."

"It ain't de shoe?"

"Hell, no. Not these here shoes." He put his hands on them. "Looka there—sof' as a glove. Plenty big too; see? It's de damn sock."

Terry did not argue, but he was unconvinced.

"You railroadin'?" the yellow boy asked.

Terry shook his head. "Nah. You?"

"Hm. It's de life. Ma daddy was a railroadin' man too."

Then he introduced himself to Terry: Napoleon Haide.

"They calls me Nappy for shawt," he said. "I'm jes' heah two days this trip. Nice gals out heah."

"You lak 'em?"

"When I says they is right, they is *right*. I done seen 'em all, from heah to New Yawk."

Terry saw that Nappy's hair and skin were near the same yellow color—what the Negroes call "riney." He had heavy lips, a thick nose, and gray eyes which were inclined to be pink around the edges. His hair, moreover, was very kinky.

"De brown-skinned gal 'cross yonder," Nappy pointed—"is she yo' company?"

"Yea, I got two," Terry said.

After that the four of them got together, a sort of party to themselves. When Nappy danced his head bent forward above the girl's and even his shoulders seemed to fold around her. Terry thought he was trying to get too much from a dance; he was too avid. But Azilee enjoyed dancing with him, and evidently her thoughts were not the same as Terry's.

VI

IN THE MIDST OF THE NOISY WHIRL, THE
gay laughter of the young people, the extrava-
gant clothes, when the young folks were least
prepared for such a surprise, Augie adjusted his
hat and entered the dance pavilion. He stood in
the doorway quietly for a moment in his ancient
and ruined finery, casting his glances about. He
wore the Prince Albert with the vest of faded
flowers and with these a pair of outlandish old
shoes for which he had improvised laces of red
ribbons. He felt arrogant and self-assured, not in
the least ashamed, and showed only scorn for the
crowd.

Seeing him standing there, Terry and Beulah
came across to him at the close of the dance.

"I thought this thing was fancy," Augie
sneered.

"Don't you lak it?" Beulah laughed.

"I'm used to fancy niggers, niggers whut would make dis crowd look 'shamed."

"That was when you was a jockey?"

"Hm. An' clo'es! I don't see no clo'es. This heah is a country ring-play. This ain't no dance."

Augie had alcohol on his breath, but he was not drunk. He, of course, was unable to take part in the modern dances. His scorn would not have permitted it anyway.

"I got de hoss an' wagon," he said. "It outside waitin' for you, Miss Beulah. I'll drive y'all gals home when you is through dancin'."

"Thank you, Lil Augie."

"Whut 'bout me?" Terry smiled.

"You an' Miss Azilee betta walk," Augie said. "Y'all betta walk. Me an' Miss Beulah might wanna co't." He punched Terry with his elbow.

In the dances that followed, Terry stood up often in order to keep Augie company. He must have imagined that the old man felt as out of place as he looked. The crowd increased steadily, and the circle became uncomfortably compact. Revolving slowly, it suggested a gaudy pinwheel. Augie amused himself by watching the couples.

A muscular black girl went by in a sleeveless dress and striped stockings. Others followed: a buff-colored girl with a face painted till it resembled porcelain, a short dwarfed girl with incongruous hands and feet dancing with a tall man, a young buck with rubber hips and a distressed woman who held his neck, a bold pair who stood in a shadow writhing, a beautiful brown girl yielding the curves of her body to a hideous-looking man, a stout woman whose preposterous breasts kept her partner at a safe distance.

"Bumpety-bump," some one sang.

"Ah buggie-wuggie!"

Many were perspiring. There was a steady hum of voices. Some place in the mass a woman shouted.

"Oo-wee!"

It was an odd outburst, not unlike those uttered in religious frenzy. A few girls giggled. Most of them were too absorbed even to notice.

Augie saw Terry, dancing with Beulah again, weaving deftly through the compact crowd near the orchestra. Suddenly in the midst of the caldron something hit the floor with a thump like a dead weight. In the center of a little clearing was the fat woman whom Terry had seen during the afternoon. She was sprawled on the slick floor and laboring with the aid of three men to regain her feet, but those high-heeled shoes were gigantic handicaps. Her little sheepish escort babied her a moment, and they set out again bravely.

Directly in front of the musicians there was a bit of space where the floor was brighter than elsewhere because of the extra lights for the orchestra. Some of the dancers were inclined to hurry past this spot because it put them too much in evidence. Others sought it and lingered there, passing remarks with the musicians. A flashy pair were showing a new dance that they had picked up in the city, on Central Avenue, in some of the less respectable places, and were attracting considerable attention. It was a dance in which the shoulders and hips twitched rhythmically, but in which the feet made no steps.

Couples, seeing them, exchanged meaning glances. Some of the men said things that made the girls giggle.

"Jelly! A-ah jelly! Jelly on a plate!"

"Slow an' easy."

"Now rock lak a boat."

The denizens of Mudtown were seeing the shimmy for the first time in a public place. In those days it was regarded as a low, unseemly dance, and the young country girls felt a little outraged at seeing it done there so boldly. Terry, too, seemed embarrassed and kept trying to work through the crowd, to get a safe distance away.

But Augie watched it calmly from the sidelines. He had nothing but scorn for the modern nigger dances. He thought of the night he walked with Della Green at the Cotton Flower Ball. That had been a real come-off. That was what he called a dance. It was fancy.

Nappy's own girl, a hard-looking scrawny wench with broken front teeth, had been neglected and was now looking for him. Seeing her, Nappy excused himself from his new acquaintances and went where she was standing. The dance was about played out; people were leaving. Terry called Azilee, and with Augie and Beulah they left.

The moon was big outside. Everything else seemed small—the trees, the houses, and the little blue hills in the distance. Augie and Beulah got in the cart, and Augie clucked at Miss Ludy.

The tiny rig wavered and jolted along a white-washed fence, beneath overhanging branches, and turned into the big road.

Terry and Azilee followed a footpath to the road. After the poorly ventilated pavilion and the reek of perspiring dancers, the night air was a blessing. As they walked Terry watched the cart. He could almost cry looking at Augie in his ridiculous mashed-up hat sitting beside Beulah!

A block away the sound of the bleating horns reached them, faint and shrunken like a thing remembered. There was, of course, no pavement in the neighborhood and only a single street lamp above the low houses. With this behind, tall incredible shadows fell before Terry and Azilee, creeping face downward as they walked.

Some one ahead on the path laughed merrily, another couple leaving. Arm in arm the fat mulattress and her slight black companion had forgotten pain. Her shoes tied together and suspended across her shoulder, she padded along comfortably in stockinged feet.

VII

LISSUS, WHO HAD BEEN AWAY ON ONE OF those periodic absences, returned to his hut a few days after the Green Lake Dance, and for the first time Augie got a glimpse of the lean easygoing black.

It was midsummer. The sugar beet harvest was approaching. The wide acres of the level countryside quivered with a shimmering transparent green. The fruit trees were overloaded. Props had been placed beneath the apple boughs to keep them from breaking under the burden. Tisha and the Clow girls were in the field, pulling fodder and topping the full-grown corn.

The two men met in the road.

"So you's Lil Augie?" Lissus said.

"Lil Augie whut you reads about! There ain't but de one."

"I ain't read 'bout no Lil Augie."

Augie sneered. " 'Course not. You wa'n't heah in ma time. I'm ole nuff to be yo' damn daddy."

"Be ma daddy, lak hell! You might be ole nuff, but you ain't never seen de day you could be ma daddy. No lil ole sumpin' lak you. You ain't had de nachal man-power."

"Lissen to me, black boy. I been a man. I been sweet papa to womens whut wouldn't spit on de bes' part o' you. Don't tell me 'bout whut I ain't been!"

"Maybe so. Maybe you *been* a man, Lil Augie. You ain't none no mo'."

"I be dog if I ain't. Lil Augie is damn-it-to-hell yet. An' any nigger whut thinks it ain't so can jes' try me a barrel."

"Wha, wha! Would you fight, Lil Augie?"

"You heared me."

"You hell wid de womens too?"

But Augie had turned his back on the tall ragged fellow and had started down the road, chewing on his pipe and kicking up dust. There was scorn in every step he took, in every breath of smoke he blew. Lissus was a low nigger in his eyes (a hideous nobody, compared with the Little

Augie people used to read about), and he hated him because of it. Besides, Lissus was Tisha's man, and that alone was enough to sink him hopelessly in Augie's opinion.

That evening a freight train dropped a string of box cars on a rusty side-rail in front of the Clows' place. Seeing them the next morning, Augie was reminded again of the nearing harvest. The cars formed a wall between Leah's house and the Clows'. In one way Augie thought this a good thing—it would keep Tisha and Lissus out of his eyes for a few days. But he promptly recognized it also as an inconvenience. He had awakened with Beulah on his mind, and he had hoped to step to his door and perhaps catch sight of her in the high field or on the embankment. She and Azilee were usually out early these days. He had intended to get her eye by waving his hat and to give her a good "howdy." But the box cars spoiled that. So Augie just sighed and turned his back on his disappointment. Instead he gathered up his wooden pails and went down to the pump to draw water for the heifers, which by now were lowing at the gate, their slimy noses resting on the top piece.

All morning Augie kept steadily at his work. By noon the pigs were contentedly buried in their mud, their stomachs stuffed with corn and kitchen swill. The pigeons were in the air, wheeling in great circles, exercising their wings. The heifers were lying in the corner of their yard under a lemon verbena tree, drowsing and chewing their cud, while Miss Ludy stood in the bright sunshine like a miserable old creature from a funny paper, her bones projecting grotesquely and her shaggy head hanging. A plague of flies were tormenting her, but she was too sleepy to resent them; she didn't even twitch her tail.

Seeing her there, Augie suddenly suspected that his design to breed a race horse from her was hopelessly impossible. But he was not quite ready to admit that, even to himself. He had not given up the project but merely deferred it because of more immediate business. Beulah was on his mind.

A little later, in the afternoon, he put on his Sunday clothes, his long coat, the fancy vest, and the top-hat and started across the railroad to call on the girls. Since he had no pants or shoes or shirt to match, he did not bother to change these. Yet he did put a collar button at the collarless throat of his old shirt and strung his shoes with the improvised red ribbon laces he had worn to the dance.

He crawled under the box cars and came out on the other side, slapping his hips and dusting himself like a partridge. Then he wavered down the path, through the clump of castor-bean trees, and timidly knocked at the front door of the tiny whitewashed shack. While he stood waiting he heard the girls giggling in the big room; he smelt the odors of Clara Clow's kitchen, the delicious hog meat boiling in her kettles.

After a moment Clara came to the door, wiping her face with her apron. She pulled an old rocker out and invited Augie to have some sit-down.

" 'Scuse me, Lil Augie," she said. "I can't stay out with you 'cause I got ma dinner on de fire."

"Don't mind me, Miss Clara. I's jes' home folks. Business comes 'fo' chewin' de rag. Where's them ole sassy gals o' yourn at?"

"He, he! They's inside, Lil Augie. They ain't a bit o' good. Was they worth a dime I wouldn't have to do no cookin'."

"These young uns is one mo' mess nowadays. De doctor can't do 'em no good."

"Tha's a prayer, Lil Augie."

"They done got me all spry an' devilish too."

"Hush, Lil Augie," she laughed. "You's too ole to kick up yo' heels any mo'."

"Me? Miss Clara, I's worser'n a lil ole bull. I's so bad I hits at maself in de lookin'-glass."

"He, he! Beulah, you betta come heah an' do sumpin' wid dis lil ole man." She started toward the kitchen. " 'Scuse me, Lil Augie. De gals'll be heah directly."

Augie crossed his legs and rocked. There was a slight stir of air. A few crisp leaves rattled in the yard. Occasionally one fell, a great golden flake. For some reason Augie kept thinking of the day he called on Florence after the memorable season in St. Louis. Perhaps it was because that afternoon, like this one, had come at the end of the summer, because there had been brown leaves falling like flakes through the yellow sunlight.

Times had changed, Augie thought. And despite the pain through which he had passed, the miles he had journeyed, and the years he had waited, life was no better. He had become poorer and poorer. There was little indeed left of the bright clothes he had worn in those days. Now, of course, for the moment, things looked more attractive. Beulah was in his mind, but he did not fool himself into really believing that Beulah could be compared with Florence or that these surroundings were as pleasant as those in which he had courted that fancy yellow gal. Those days, those surroundings, were long gone.

Augie refilled his pipe and toyed with the red laces in his ridiculous oversized shoes. In spite of his general wretchedness, this single touch of color seemed to give him a curious pleasure. He had no idea of the reason. Augie continued to rock. And while he rocked the moments passed and the girls delayed.

But Augie was not impatient as young people are in love. He did not suspect that the girls were inside, laughing at him. His mind was so full of pictures he could amuse himself for hours, if need be, without noticing the passage of time. So when they did finally come out Augie was, for just an instant, almost irritated to have them break into his thoughts.

Beulah sat on the steps in her clean gingham

dress, and Azilee went out beneath the trees to pick a few apples. The girls smacked their lips noisily on the firm juicy fruit. Augle peeled his with his pocket knife and cut them into thin slices. His teeth were not equal to biting a hard apple.

Suddenly it occurred to Augie that the sun was low, that it was nearing the time for him to feed the pigs and heifers. He had spent all his time waiting for the girls to come out, and there wasn't any left for visiting.

"I was jes' gonna ask y'all gals could you come cross de line tomorrow night. Leah an' me's gonna make some 'lasses balls an' one thing an' anuther. She wants y'all to come help Terry eat 'em up. An' we can play some music."

"Oh, sho', Lil Augie," Beulah said.

"Tha's good. I got to go now."

"A'ready?"

Augie rolled his eyes playfully. "Don't look at me lak dat. I feels ma love comin' down. I'm apt to haul off an' bite ma name in yo' jaws."

The girls giggled.

"Would you bite a gal jes' cause o' dat?"

"I'm bad," Augie said. "You don't know me yet."

"Maybe I don't care if you is bad, Lil Augie. Maybe I don't much care if you do bite ma jaw."

"Well, I done got you tole. I'm bad when ma love start to comin' down."

That evening after supper Augie was walking up and down the middle of the road, plowing his feet in the deep dust and enjoying his pipe and his thoughts. He was wondering how Beulah had been impressed by his sassy words, if she had been shrewd enough to guess that beneath his mock playfulness he was in dead earnest. He had been forced to put his sentiments in the form of a joke because he had found no opportunity to speak them in private and directly.

Presently the road became dark and two tall shadowy figures jumped out of an open box car, ran down the embankment to the road, and almost trampled Little Augie. They were just a few feet from him when they turned and went in the opposite direction. Of course, with his defective eyes, he could not make them out in the darkness, but Augie heard their voices and they were very familiar. It was also apparent that they

recognized him, for the girl gave a short frightened cry when first she confronted him and
turned quickly away, while the man laughed out
proudly and seemed on the verge of speaking to
Augie.

"M-m-m," Augie grieved. "If it ain't Beulah an'
Lissus."

He turned and watched their long thin shadows receding in the road. They seemed so young
and spry and mischievous, slipping around the
string of cars, he could not, at first, get deeply
angry. He only felt disappointed, as if he had lost
something. But gradually, as Lissus' disgusting
image slowly returned to his mind, Augie became
bitter.

"Well, damn his black mammy an' all his kin-
folks. An' damn dat ole cawn-fiel' gal, damn her
too. Dis is de beatin'est thing ever I seed. I
thought dat gal had taste."

Then suddenly Augie repented of his words.
Maybe he had misjudged Beulah. His eyes were
so poor in the dark that he had no right to trust
them. On second thought he was not at all sure
the two had been in the box car; they might have
simply been trying to cross the tracks by squeez-

ing between the cars instead of going around as they afterward did.

The uncertainty made him sad.

"I got de down-yonders," he said. "I got de down-yonders, an' I got 'em bad. If I wa'n't so devilish ole an' ugly an' black I'd jes' bus' out an' cry. Oo-wee! Womens ain't nuthin' but a worry-ation to a man's mind—from de time he check in to de time he check out. I got de down-yonders, an' I'm too damn mean to cry."

VIII

THE NEXT EVENING AUGIE AND LEAH
made a large pan of the old-fashioned popcorn
and molasses balls they had promised the young
folks. Azilee and Beulah sat with Terry and Leah
at the table, and Augie pulled his chair into a corner and began limbering up his accordion. While
he was playing and the others eating popcorn
and listening quietly, a little hoot owl alighted
on a fence post outside and set up a soft, mourn-
ful recitation. Leah stood in the middle of the
floor, panic-stricken. Her eyes glowing with terror, she angled her ear to hear it again.

She turned to Augie with a frightened whisper.

"Looka yonder. Ain't dat ma ole shoe behind
de stove?"

Augie gave the shoe a kick but didn't stop
playing.

"Turn it up, Terry," the old woman said. "Quick."

Then she hurried to the door and began sprinkling salt on the ground.

"How come you do that?" Beulah asked.

"Make him go way. Owl hootin' mean bad day comin'."

The owl went away, but Leah was troubled the rest of the evening. The girls became frightened, and Augie had to walk home with them. When he came back he wanted to play some more music, but Leah said no. So he and Terry sat and talked. They were unable to draw Leah into the conversation, however. Terry had seen his grandmother fighting bad luck before, crossing sticks and burning hair, and Augie had understood and obeyed the signs all his natural life. But no harm ever threatened Leah's home; so these things had come to receive only a small attention. This time, however, Augie and Terry were both impressed. That devilish little owl sounded bad outside on the fence post, terribly bad.

Summer was definitely passed. The heavy, unpruned trees, overburdened with fruit, were touching the ground. A crimson rambler that covered the side of Leah's barn and a portion of the adjoining barnyard fence showered the place with petals. Weeds had taken the garden, and the dry grass was knee-deep along the roadside.

A day or two later the beet harvest began. Before sunrise a large revolving plow drawn by a double team of iron-gray horses was in the field. It turned two furrows at a time and left the sugar beets on the ground in precise rows. It was a good crop. And now that the devastation had commenced, the fading green of the fields seemed even more striking than before.

The toppers, a gang of Mexicans, arrived an hour or two later. Passing Augie at his gate, some of them greeted him in their own language. He smiled and mumbled an answer without committing himself to any particular tongue.

They were men with grave, humorless faces, bountiful mustaches, and eyes the expressions of which Augie could not interpret. They carried long, heavy knives like butcher's tools. Holding the beets by the points, they were able to slice away the top leaves accurately with one stroke.

They took their places at the head of the rows, side by side, and began a steady march across the wide acres abreast, throwing the tops aside and leaving the beets in orderly piles.

Meanwhile there was also much work to be done on Leah's place. Most of it fell to Terry. Augie, having learned the way to Watts, continued to drink so heavily that he could not be depended upon to look after the chores, much less the picking of the apples, the sweet-potato digging, or the shocking of the corn.

Leah had tried to break his habit by putting little odd fish in his whiskey. Folks said that liquor thus prepared would turn a drinker away from his bottle forever. It would revolt him so he could never afterward bear the taste of whiskey. So Leah had tried it in all earnestness on Augie. But he took the doctored liquor without blinking an eye. Something, to be sure, was wrong with the taste of it, but not enough, apparently, to discourage Augie's fond love. His money was limited; yet he found ways of getting enough to allow him an occasional excursion to Watts.

Discouraged by her failure, Leah refused to permit Augie to remain around the house when he was intoxicated. She would give him a lunch in a tin pail and rush him off toward the barn. He invariably continued on to the swamp.

One day when Terry had worked late and was having supper after dark, Beulah and Tisha came in to sit and talk awhile. They remained so long that Leah coaxed them to eat also. Before they had finished the door banged open and Augie stumbled through. He had been in the swamp and was spattered with mud. A scar on his cheek was bleeding slowly and his eyes shone.

Leah went to the stove, quite unconcerned, and began washing her pots. She didn't even look up from the dishpan.

"Get up from dat table, every damn one o' you, an' let me sit down." He turned to Leah directly: "Feed me, gal."

"Hush dat mouf," she said quietly. "You mind me of a alligator."

"I'm gonna eat, by Gawd."

"Maybe you is, maybe you ain't," Leah mused.

Tisha frowned and said: "Mind out how you talk, Lil Augie. 'Member you's drunk."

Augie's little falsetto shrieked.

"I won't take a insult off'n you, woman. You

ain't so big. An' damn if you's gonna low-rate me in ma own house. Damn if you is."

No one answered Augie again. Leah talked aloud to herself: "Beulah's ole pappy oughta could be 'live to heah dat. . . . Cussin' an' goin' on lak a crazy 'fo' his gal. Dat ole man woulda wringed yo' monstrous neck for you."

"We'd jes' have a fight," Augie said. "Tha's all."

"That you would."

Augie's manner became suave.

"Bes' man win," he said.

As usual, after his wild remarks, Augie looked pitiful. The young folks had seemed a little frightened when he broke through the door, but now the little man looked as absurd as an infant, talking of fighting a real full-sized man. A hopeless old wreck, Augie still had dreams of heroism too big for his body. In his drunkenness the sizes of things became temporarily adjusted.

Augie withdrew far more quietly than he had come. From the window the folks heard him making his way with considerable effort on the gravel path to the road. When Beulah and Tisha were returning home, Terry followed them out to the gate. A short distance away, on the railroad tracks, he saw Augie stumbling about as if searching for something he had lost and talking aloud to himself.

Some moving clouds shadowed the moon like enormous wings; it was going to rain. Half a mile down the road a streak of light was traveling: some one carrying a lantern. There was the rattle and hum of a windmill in motion and, on the air, the oppressive sweetness of dying vines.

Tisha had been silent for some time. Outside the gate she said: "He one o' dem lil hard-bottom niggers! I gonna show him sumpin' one o' dese days."

"Don't mind Augie," Terry said. "He's gentle as a kitten; that whiskey talk don't mean nuthin'."

"Maybe it don't mean nuthin'," she said. "But it can sho' get him a heap o' trouble." She shifted the tobacco in her mouth and spat.

"I don't know how come he keeps on drinkin' so bad," Terry said. "We had some plans, but it look lak he done forgot all about 'em."

Tisha grunted but did not speak. Beulah was afraid that Augie might really try to hurt some one.

"Y'all betta mind out when he's lak dat," she told Terry.

Tisha butted in: "He gonna forgit an' cuss somebody whut's jes' as bad as him one o' dese days. When he do he gonna get mashed up."

When the two were gone Terry stood at the gate a moment and tried to imagine why Tisha hated Augie so bitterly. It seemed impossible for any one to hate such a tiny, gentle old person. He scratched his head and walked back to the house. As he reached the door some raindrops blew in his face.

An hour or two afterward, sleeping on a cot near the door, Terry was awakened by a sudden sharp knocking. A pause followed; then it recommenced, and he heard Augie's voice calling outside Leah's window.

"Leah! Ah, Leah!"

Leah did not answer. Outside the rain continued on the crisped fruit trees. A little tremor ran over Terry's flesh. Augie's wounded voice, coming unexpected out of the dark, suggested a ghost. Terry raised himself nervously on his elbow.

"Ma Leah," he called in a whisper.

"Whut dat, son?"

"Augie's locked out. He can't get in his room."

"Let him stay out," she said, unmoved. "Learn him a lesson."

It seemed like harsh discipline on such a night. But Leah was wide awake, and Terry knew that she meant what she said. The wind had increased, and a tree limb brushed the house occasionally. Presently Augie returned and rapped against the house again.

"Whut you want?" Leah called.

"I wanna come in an' sleep," Augie said. "De do' is locked."

"You ain't comin' in heah dis night, not drunk as you is."

"Where's I gonna sleep?"

"Bes' place you can," Leah said. "There's a great big ole barn out yonder. You can sleep wid de cows."

Augie protested a moment feebly. "I ain't drunk," he kept on saying.

But Leah refused to answer again. He came once more to the door and tried to kick it open. Then he went away. Terry could hear him plop-plopping in the mud, still muttering to himself as he left.

IX

Oh, de jack won't drink muddy water
An' he won't back off.

AUGIE WAS NOT REAL DRUNK, JUST PLEAS-
antly mellow. He had on a clean blue shirt with a
scarlet handkerchief at the throat for a tie. Sitting
on the front doorsteps, he indolently fingered his
accordion. Inside, Leah's creaking rocker could be
heard rhythmically between pauses.

De boat's gone up de river
An' de tide's gone down.

In the level adjoining fields the beet harvest
was finished. A herd of Texas steers had been
brought in to fatten on the tops that were left on
the ground. They were lean untamed animals

with incredible horns and were tended by cow-
boys and dogs in the old romantic manner familiar to readers of western fiction. Augie watched
them wistfully as he sang.

> I'm goin' to de nation an' marry me an'
>   Injun squaw,
> An' let some Injun woman be ma mother-
>   in-law.

For a week or two Augie had been himself
again. Since the rainy night in the barn he had
not been thoroughly intoxicated. He was happy
once more with his designs to breed a race horse
and give the heifers a proper raising. A neighbor-
ing farmer had given him permission to drive
over his fields with the democrat wagon and
glean the residue of beets missed by his own
automatic plows or dropped from his wagons.
They made excellent food for the milk cow, and
Augie managed to find several loads. They would
all come in handy during the winter.

Augie's improved behavior was a great relief to
Leah's mind. She could sit quietly during the
afternoon and enjoy her pipe. If he had only

with round child eyes, exhausted and dismayed. No one spoke.

Later that morning when Augie had fed the stock, he went to a bench to chop a few sugar beets for the cow. He used a beet knife similar to the ones used by the Mexicans in topping. As he worked he recalled a few verses from the old St. Louis boogie-house songs and sang them loudly in order to drive the morning's experience out of his mind. That was a familiar trick with him.

The old cow came to the gate, and raising her head above the bar, uttered a prolonged impatient word. Two heifers drew near and stood beside her. From the distance Augie could hear the pigs squealing in the marsh. He finished chopping and began to scoop the beets into a wooden pail.

> *Got full o' moonshine, walked de streets*
>   *all night,*
> *Got full o' moonshine, walked de streets*
>   *all night,*
> *Squabblin' wid ma black gal 'cause she*
>   *wasn't white.*

"Wha', wha'," a voice laughed. "You is mighty happy for sich a *ole* man."

Augie looked up into the hideous, unshaven face of Lissus. The latter was barefooted and wore only his threadbare pants and the red flannel undershirt. He was leaning with one foot on the fence, and his thick lips hung loosely apart. Augie spat in disgust.

"Go on off an' lay down, nigger. Was I as black an' ugly as you I'd waller wid de hogs 'stead o' 'sociatin' wid folkses."

"Tha's yo' burr, ole man. You don't know papa Lissus—black an' greasy an' sweet to de womens."

"Sweet to hell. Sweet to dat black-cat Tisha an' them ole battleships round yonder by de swamp. Nuthin' whut's equal to a stray dog could 'bide dat codfish smell o' yourn."

"Miss Beulah think I'm sweet too."

Augie was silent a moment. Then a quick fire came into his eyes.

"Damn yo' black mammy, nigger. I'm a-mind to lump you for dat lie."

"Them's fightin' words, Lil Augie."

"Lil Augie is a fightin' man, Mistah Lissus."

"You think it ain't so, hunh?"

"Say it again an' I'll whup yo' ears down, Mistah Lissus."

"Whut you 'spect us was doin' in dat box car de other evenin'—countin' pennies?"

Augie flew into Lissus' face like a wild bird and quickly slapped both fists to the larger fellow's face. Lissus' lip was split by the blows. A tiny stream of blood curled from the corner of his mouth. He calmly stepped over the low fence.

"I guess tha's ma fightin' piece, ole man."

Augie came back again, both fists flying. Lissus shook him off as if he were a child and countered with a sharp side-arm blow. His fist, inscribing a perfect semicircle, caught Augie on the left ear. At the same instant the small man's feet went out from under him, and he hit the ground like a ninepin.

From the ground, through a dense haze, he caught sight of Lissus before him in a menacing stance. He was shouting, but Augie could not hear his words. With a pronounced effort Augie succeeded in drawing himself up by the bench. Then light seemed to break. His fingers moved toward the beet knife. Seeing this gesture, Lissus came at him again.

Augie waved the long shiny blade insanely above his head, chattering like a little ape-man, then brought it downward with every ounce of his weight. Lissus staggered a moment, then sank to the ground.

A moment he rolled in the dirt like a speared hog, but after that he seemed to regain some of his strength and pulled himself to his feet. His face and hands and the front of his clothes were plastered with blood.

Augie awakened to what he had done and groaned.

"Did I hu't you, big nigger?"

"Hm, lil nigger," Lissus moaned. "You hu't me bad."

Lissus wabbled a moment on his unsteady legs and set out through Leah's little orchard toward his own hut. Augie watched him sadly—the wretched figure staggering beneath the young fruit trees, falling from limb to limb, grabbing and steadying himself by their support. Augie saw him toiling in the bright sunlight like a drunken man, making an insane effort to reach the road. The soft ground was a handicap; to the bleeding Lissus it was like struggling in a bog. To

Augie it seemed that Lissus would never make it. At every moment he expected to see the big fellow collapse. Augie was still resting against the fence, paralyzed. He felt like a man in a nightmare. He closed his eyes and tried to collect his thoughts.

When he opened them Lissus had miraculously crossed the road. He was on his hands and knees, trying to pull himself up the railroad embankment. A moment or two later he reached the top and then disappeared on the other side.

A flight of fan-tailed pigeons alighted on the low barn roof and began a dull chant. The sun went higher and brighter. One of the glossy heifers rubbed Augie's arm with her wet nose. The old cow was still waiting for her beets.

X

AUGIE SAT ON THE EDGE OF HIS COT, tossing shoes, old shirts, and underclothes into the badly used wicker traveling-bag. It was leaving-time again.

"I thought I was fixed for life," he said. "But I ain't stayed heah no longer'n I stayed anywhere else."

He finished packing and put on the little greasy dirt-colored vest that once had been milk-white with red roses. But he decided not to wear the coat; so he folded it carefully and laid it across the other rags in his bag. A moment later he gathered up his luggage, the bag in one hand, the accordion in the other, and slipped out beneath the trees of the yard.

Night had fallen, and the moon was up, glimmering white, remote and sadlike. The garden corn had been shocked and stood near the fence in little abandoned wigwams. Augie's heart was full of misery.

"I done carved ole Lissus wid de beet knife," he said. "I done carved him good an' I'm glad I done it. He over yonder now strugglin' in his blood. An' he might be dead. So it's leavin'-time for Lil Augie. Leavin'-time, an' I ain't comin' back."

He paused a moment, leaning on the gate post, chewing the stem of his pipe with toothless gums. The dusty road was white in the moonlight and seemed to curve upward at the end where it went out of sight. Augie crossed it slowly and began climbing the railroad embankment. Standing between the tracks, he gazed first in one direction and then in the other. Both seemed alike from where he stood. At each end there was a dim shining point. One way was familiar to Augie—it was the way by which he had come to Mudtown only a few short weeks earlier. The other way was new and strange. That was the way he chose to go.

He began walking slowly. Beyond the high weeds, nesting in a clump of red castor-bean trees, he saw the Clow shack. Farther away, across the white sandy pasture, was the hut of Lissus and Tisha. Beulah was in one of those houses. But Augie kept on walking. Behind him on the other side of the road Leah and Terry were sitting in their tiny kitchen with no idea of what had happened, no idea that Augie was leaving.

"I done lef' 'em lak a dream," he said. "I'm goin' to Tia Juana, an' I ain't gonna write no letter."

Suddenly Augie heard footsteps under the low fruit trees on the Clows' place. He paused a moment and heard his heart thumping. He saw no one. Still the footsteps kept coming. They were coming toward him.

A moment later Tisha stepped out from the shadows, climbed the barbed-wire fence, and started up the embankment a distance behind Augie. Her head was tied in a handkerchief, her skirts were tucked above her knees, and she was wearing a pair of heavy man's shoes. She had in her hand the blacksnake with which she drove the mules, and her cheeks were swollen with chewing-tobacco.

Augie had time to wonder what she was doing

on the railroad tracks at that hour—considering
the condition of Lissus. But he promptly realized
that she was following him. He began to speed
his steps. Tisha was after him with the mule
whip. She was after him for hitting Lissus with
the beet knife. Her steps were steady and deliber-
ate. Yet she seemed to Augie to be drawing closer
and closer to him. He was now walking as fast as
his legs would carry him. But it wasn't fast
enough. He began to run.

Suddenly the wicker bag went off the handle,
fell open and tumbled down the side of the
embankment. Augie saw at a glance that his rags
were scattered among the dry stalks of wild mustard, his Prince Albert was hung on a briar.

"Tha's de las' button on Gabriel's coat," he
muttered sadly. "Tha's eve'thing I got."

Tisha was still following, still threatening him
with the whip; so he could not stop to regain his
possessions. Instead he added speed to his steps.

A moment later, however, a wave of shame
passed over him, and he stopped dead still in his
tracks.

"Whut done got in me?" he said. "Heah I is
breakin' ma neck runnin' from a woman—dat

stinkin' black cat Tisha. Dis ain't lak Lil Augie. Dis ain't me."

Tisha had turned back. Augie could see her between the rails. She now seemed tiny and far away in the moonlight.

Augie rubbed his head. His hat too was gone. The night air felt cool on his bald spot. He chewed the stem of his cob pipe and realized that it was dry. The pipe was lost; it had fallen from the stem.

"I ain't nobody. I ain't nuthin'," he said. "I's jes' a po' picked sparrow. I ain't big as a dime, an' I don't worth a nickel."

But there was no need to turn back. He had carved Lissus with the beet knife, and it was leaving-time. He wasn't tired, and he still had his accordion. Tia Juana was somewhere ahead. He had learned that much from the postman. And there, he had been told, there was horse racing and plenty of liquor.

A few moments later a big locomotive headlight rose above the dim horizon and flashed in Augie's face. He left the embankment and got in the middle of the road. As the train drew nearer he could tell by its labored pulling that it was heavily loaded. The whole countryside, a tiny dark world with its near-by horizon, trembled at its approach. The trees rocked; fences swayed.

At a crossroads Augie stopped and waited for the long freighter to pass. While he stood there a large motor truck drove up and stopped beside him.

Some one shouted from the seat, "Where you goin', governor?"

" 'Way down de line," Augie said. "To Tia Juana."

"Hop on if you wanna."

"Yes, *suh!*"

When the train finished passing, the truck pulled across the tracks and opened up on the smooth gravel road of the opposite side. Augie stretched out on the floor, resting his head on a pile of sacks, and began limbering up his accordion.

> *Oh de boat's gone up de river*
> *An' de tide's gone down.*

The night air whizzed about his head. Trees and houses and hills were flying past him like leaves in a hurricane. A little democrat wagon went by like a mere pasteboard toy. A strangely familiar feeling of exhilaration came to Augie, an illusion that came with speed. When had he felt that thrill before? He recalled Mr. Woody and his fast horses. It had been a good many years. So many indeed that Augie could not remember.

Epilogue

The Givens Foundation for African American Literature

You have to know where you came from to understand where you are going. This familiar expression of the value of history speaks to the heart of the Givens Foundation for African American Literature. Our partnership with Washington Square Press to republish out-of-print African American classics helps accomplish a long-held goal of keeping literature and its lessons alive.

The Givens Foundation is devoted to enriching cultural understanding through programs that advance and celebrate African American literature. Our programs are inspired by and designed to serve the Archie Givens, Sr., Collection of African American Literature at the University of Minnesota's Elmer L. Andersen Library. The collection includes over 9,000 books, pamphlets, manuscripts, letters, and ephemera representing more than two centuries of African American cultural accomplishments. Many of these items are signed, rare, and first-edition volumes. Each year hundreds of books, ranging from novels, plays, poems, short stories, and autobiographies to nonfiction and scholarly titles, join the collection.

While the University holds these historical artifacts for future generations in a secure environment, the Givens Foundation keeps their content alive through programs for contemporary audiences: readings, discussion forums, exhibits, conferences, and "teach the teacher" programs for educators seeking African American literary resources for the classroom.

The Givens Collection Classics series, from which you hold just one volume, unveils powerful stories and expressions from generations gone by. We believe that our past informs and shapes both our present and future. It is our profound hope that a new generation of readers will discover these books and gain a deeper understanding of our rich and multifaceted American history. We hope that you have enjoyed reading this book and will share it with others. Please let us know.

Archie Givens, Jr.
President
Givens Foundation for
African American Literature

7151 York Avenue South
Minneapolis, MN 55435
(952) 831-2555
www.givens.org

For information about the Givens Collection at the University of Minnesota, contact:

Special Collections and Rare Books
111 Elmer L. Andersen Library
222 21st Avenue South
Minneapolis, MN 55455
(612) 624-3855
http://special.lib.umn.edu/rare/givens/